Getting Played

Celeste O. Norfleet

Recycling programs
for this product may
not exist in your area.

GETTING PLAYED

ISBN-13: 978-0-373-53432-6

www.KimaniTRU.com

Printed in U.S.A.

Acknowledgments

As always, to Charles, my love, my heart and my best friend forever—thank you for always being here for me. Also, much love to Christopher and Jennifer. You make this so much fun. I couldn't have done this without you.

I'd also like to thank my teens of the heart, Theo, Sasha and Vanessa Salnave and Michael, Christian and Amanda Siler—even though you're miles away, know that you're always right here in my heart.

To my postteens—Charles and Prince and my very preteens, Damiah, Aniah and Charles, thank you for bringing so much joy into my world.

Special thanks to my sisters, Amanda Mitchell and Karen Linton. You are so special to me and a true blessing to my heart. To my mother, Mable Johnson, thank you for keeping me inspired and reminding me what I was like as a teenager.

To my sisters of the heart, Francis DeLoach, Andrea Jenkins, Paulette Jones, Michelle Monkou, Candice Poarch, Renee Salnave and Suzi White. Thank you for surrounding me with your knowledge, wisdom and positive energy.

Much love to the extraordinary women who keep me going and remind me that I can do anything. You never cease to amaze me. To my exceptionally talented editor Evette Porter—you are brilliant! Thank you for challenging me and making me better than I ever imagined I could be. To my wonderful agent Elaine English—you're a lifesaver. Thank you for always being there with words of encouragement when all I can see is a blank monitor page. Also, much thanks to Naomi Hackenberg—you're the best.

Last, but certainly not least, thank you teachers, librarians and readers. It's a joy to continue writing Kenisha Lewis's story for you. There's so much more to come.

Please feel free to write me and let me know what you think. I always enjoy hearing from readers. Please send your comments to conorfleet@aol.com or Celeste O. Norfleet, P.O. Box 7346, Woodbridge, VA 22195-7346.

Enjoy!

To Fate & Fortune

CHAPTER 1

The Way Out Is the Way In

"Goodbye. Au revoir. Adios. Arrivederci. Kwaherini. In English, French, Spanish, Italian or Swahili, it doesn't matter what language you say it in. It all means the same thing—I'm out of here."

—*MySpace.com*

HOW time passes always amazes me. When you want it to speed up, it slows down. And when you want it to slow down, it zips by in a flash. Go figure.

Right now I really need to get out of here. I'm looking at the clock on the wall and impatiently tapping my pencil on the desk. All I've been thinking about for the past nine days is putting this drama behind me. So when Ms. Grayson announces a pop quiz and then puts the test on my desk facedown, it's the last thing I expect to be doing on my final day at this school. When I turn the exam over, I silently groan: a history quiz. *Are you kidding me?* I look up at Ms. Grayson, who is engrossed in a book and already in her leave-me-the-hell-alone mode.

Name:

I scribble *Kenisha Lewis* halfheartedly at the top of the page.

Date:

Seriously, does it really matter at this point?

Class period/subject:

I write *6th period/U.S. History.*

It's my last day here and I'm finding it way too hard to keep the smirk off my face. I look up at the clock again, then back at the test I'm supposed to be completing. It's fill-in-the-blank and multiple-choice. I have no idea why teachers think history is supposed to be interesting. Who cares what a bunch of dead people did a few hundred years ago? How is this supposed to change my life right now? It's not. So why even bother?

I start writing, but lose interest by the third question. For real, right now my mind is a million miles away. I've been spacing out for the last five days. The thought of going back to my real school and my real life is all I can think about. I tap my pencil on the desk again and notice my eraser is half gone. I have to get some new pencils and some new notebooks. I also need some new clothes and sneaks. The list I'm compiling in my head is getting longer. A new backpack and a new laptop would be sweet, too. What else…

"Psst, hey, what's number two?" someone behind me whispers.

I hear someone utter the wrong answer, almost immediately trying to cover up with a very loud cough. Everyone around me starts laughing. I do, too. It's so obvious how this game is played. Still, a few seconds later someone whispers another answer. We all look at our papers to check if that's what we have. I do.

"What's number three?"

"Is there a problem back there?" Ms. Grayson says. No one responds, of course. It's an unspoken rule in high school—"snitches get stitches." So, did she really expect anyone to say, *"Yeah, somebody didn't study, so we're back here cheating our asses off."*

I look up toward the front of the class. Ms. Grayson is staring straight at me. I ignore her and look around the room at the other students in the class. I can count on one hand how many are actually paying attention. I guess we all feel pretty much the same—bored. Three months into the first semester, and it feels like I've been here a decade. I don't know if it's me or the school or what, but something's gotta give. I look up at the clock and count the minutes until I'm outta here.

For the last two weeks things have been going pretty good for me, surprisingly. I'm slowly getting my life back together. School is okay. The students around here are still lame, but that's nothing new. It's just more obvious now. It's like everybody all of a sudden is losing their mind or something. Maybe it's the weather, or the phase of the moon, the sun and the planets, or just plain stupidity. Whatever it is, it's messing with everybody's head.

But that's their drama. I'm not really paying much attention, since I expect to be out of here in a minute. By *in a minute,* I mean today. Now! As soon as possible! By here, I mean Penn Hall High School. They call it "The Penn," for obvious reasons. It looks more like a maximum security penitentiary than a high school in the middle of Washington, D.C. All the classroom windows have bars, and there are reinforced steel doors everywhere and metal detectors at every entrance. Like that's supposed to actually stop drama from happening. Seriously, you'd think with all that, we'd be safe and secure. Wrong. There was a stabbing in a fight earlier this morning. Rumor has it that one of the guys fighting had a handgun stashed in a classroom. Real safe, right? But I don't intend to be around when the rest of the drama jumps off.

I'm being paroled. These other pathetic fools have to stay here for the next year and a half or more. I sympathize. Well, not really. It just sounds good to say that. I hate most of the students here. They're either users, fakes or wannabes. Either way, I'm out of here and glad of it.

My cell phone vibrates in my jeans pocket. I choose to ignore it. I know it's probably the same stupid fool that's been blowin' up my cell all week. Somebody with half a brain thinks it's funny to call me with some dumb stuff. What, am I supposed to be scared? Hardly, it just makes it even clearer: I need to be getting up out of here.

Hazelhurst Academy for girls is all I think about now. I don't care about Chili Rodriguez or Regan Payne and my ongoing drama with them. I just want out of The Penn. Everybody's acting all weird since everything happened with Darien and the police. So what? Darien got arrested. Big deal, he should have. He deserved to. He's a thug, a dealer and a bully. They think I snitched to the police on him. I didn't have to. His girl, Sierra, already took care of that. She told, not me. But still they think it's me 'cause they can't imagine her turning on him. I can't say anything, 'cause that would be snitchin', so there it is.

I scribble a few more answers on the test paper. It's more from memory than actually studying, which I definitely didn't do. Most of this has to do with dates, names and places. I've always been good at memorization. I glanced at my notes a few minutes before the quiz was distributed. I remembered a few important names and dates, so most of it wasn't that hard.

I glance up at the clock again and see the second hand ticking a notch. I look down at the quiz on my desk and try to remember what I'm supposed to be writing, something to do with the Revolutionary War. Seriously, we're talkin' something like seventeen-whatever—who the hell cares?

As I write another answer my cell phone vibrates again. I look behind me to the left to where Cassie sits. She's chewing on her pencil not paying attention. I still can't believe she tried to mess me up like that.

"Miss Lewis?" I look to the front of the classroom. Ms. Grayson is sitting behind her desk staring at me again—this time like I have two heads or something. I look at her but don't say anything. "Kenisha." Other students start turning to look at me. I still don't say anything. "Is there a problem, Kenisha?"

"No," I finally say.

"You haven't touched your quiz."

"I'm thinking," I say firmly, giving her far less attitude than I expected, given my current mood.

"You need to get started, think and write at the same time. Class is almost over and this quiz will be reflected in

your interim grade." She glanced at the clock on the wall
then back to me. "You have fifteen minutes to finish."
Her warning is clear. She looks around to the rest of the
students, who are equally distracted, and starts droning on
about responsibility and purpose.

I glance up at the clock once more. But I see something
totally different. I see freedom. I see Hazelhurst. I tap my
pencil on the desk again waiting for her to finish her mini-
lecture. She ends by staring at me again. "You're still not
writing," she says to me.

"That's because I'm still thinking," I say slowly, enunciat-
ing each word as if she was a child. She knows my sarcasm is
intentional and so does everybody else. They start snickering
and looking at me.

"Miss Lewis, would you prefer to continue this conversation after class?" Ms. Grayson says as she glares at me.

I purse my lips together tightly and shrug. I know it's a
veiled threat, so I'm trying hard not to say anything. I just
look down at my paper. Either way it doesn't matter. There's
nothing she can say or do to me that will change anything
in my life right now. I am out of here. It's only a matter of
time.

Ms. Grayson gets up and walks down the aisle to my desk
and stands in front of me. I don't look up, but instead I tap
my pencil on the desk again. She picks up my paper and
looks at it. I smirk inside. She likes embarrassing students,
she's sadistic. It gives her a rush, probably the only thrill she
gets in her pitiful life.

She places the paper back down on my desk. She couldn't
say a thing. I'd completed the exam except for the date.

"You need to check your attitude, Miss Lewis. I'm not one of your friends, I'm your teacher," she says, her voice trailing off. I'm sure no one heard her except me. "Today is the twelfth," she adds, loudly.

"You need to get out of my face," is what I want to say to her. But I decide not to. I won't give her the satisfaction. Ms. Grayson is the type of teacher you'd expect to be cool because she's youngish and dresses nice. She likes hip-hop and acts like she knows what's up, but really she doesn't. She has major attitude most days and seems to not care at all on others. I look up. She's standing there glaring at me, looking like she's confused about something.

"I want to see you after class. Understood?"

"Fine," I say, knowing it didn't matter because I was out of here. She continues walking down the aisle, and I can hear other students around me snickering. Seriously, I am so tired of doing this. Every day it's that same stupid crap.

I just want to leave this place and go back to Hazelhurst. There, at least I'd be with my real friends, Jalisa and Diamond. For real, I need to hear something today, seriously. I took and passed the readmissions test. The letter said I got in, and the paperwork would only take a few days. It's already been two weeks. I've been counting. Nine days and six and a half hours. That's sixty-nine hours or four thousand-one-hundred-and-seventy minutes in total. I decided to stop there. I figured calculating the seconds would only depress me more.

A few minutes later somebody's ringtone starts playing. Everybody looks around and starts laughing and pointing. My heart jumps, but it isn't me, so I look around, too. It's coming from the back of the room. I turn. Cassie looks dead at me. I know she hates me now, but I really don't care. Her drama is her drama, and I'm on my way out of here.

Ms. Grayson walks over and holds her hand out for the phone. Cassie hands it over while still glaring at me as if I'm the stupid fool who called her during school hours or as if I'm the idiot who was dumb enough to leave the phone on ring and not vibrate. Everybody knows to vibrate in The Penn. Well, everybody except Cassie.

"Do we need to go through this every day, people?" Ms. Grayson asks as she walks back to the front of the class. "Your grades should be important to you. Whether you're here or somewhere else, you need to be mindful of your future. I suggest you finish up as quickly as possible."

My cell vibrates again just as the bell rings. Thank God. I'm out of here. I get up and drop my quiz on Ms. Grayson's desk. I see her talking to another student, and Cassie is waiting to get her cell phone back, so I just leave. I'm the first one out the door. "Kenisha, wait."

I hear my name and turn around. Then it hits me who was calling me—Cassie. I turn and keep going. She's got nothing to say to me. I head straight to the main office. It's my first stop every day for the past five days. All I can think about is picking up my transfer authorization and getting out of here, preferably before any more drama happens.

The new grading period starts Monday morning, so I know I'm almost out of time. I walk into the school office and look around. Students waiting there turn and look at me. They're all staring and whispering. Apparently everybody knows what happened. But they act like I'm the one who did something wrong. Stupid Darien was the one acting like a fool, and now I'm the one everybody's blaming.

I just ignore them and go over to the same student services desk I've been checking with all week. There are already three students ahead of me with various issues.

After about five minutes it's my turn. I step up to the desk. The same emaciated-looking woman with long, need-a-serious-fill acrylic nails and bad hair weave with tracks that show looks up at me. I've seen her every day this week, but still she acts like she's never seen me before. "What do you need?" she asks impatiently, like I'm disturbing her very important life or something. For real, all she has to do is answer phones, transfer calls and hand out paperwork. How hard can that be?

But fine, we've played this game for the past few days. "Umm, yeah, my name is Kenisha Lewis. I was in here yesterday. I need you to check on my transfer paperwork. It was supposed to be ready last week. I need them for Monday morning."

"What's the name of the school you're transferring to?"

"Hazelhurst Academy," I say, not seeing why she can't seem to remember all this from yesterday and the three days before that.

"In D.C.?" she asks, as if she's never heard the name before. I just asked her about it yesterday. Seriously, is she a complete idiot or what? I don't know where they get these people.

"No, Hazelhurst Academy is in Northern Virginia."

"Is it a private school?"

It's the same question she asked me yesterday. "Yes."

"Do you have an education voucher?"

"No," I said, having no idea what she's talking about.

"What's your name again?" she asks, still going through the papers in her sloppy folder. I repeat my name just as the phone on her desk rings. She grabs it and then transfers the call to another office while continuing her search for my paperwork. The phone rings again. This time, when she picks up, she smiles and laughs. She comments on the weather and somebody else whose name I don't recognize before transferring the call. She riffles through the folder a second time then looks up at me. "Okay, I'm not finding anything in here about a transfer for you. Are you sure you're supposed to transfer?" she asks.

A cold chill shoots through my body. My heart thunders. All I can think is, *are you friggin' kidding me?* Hell, yeah, I'm supposed to transfer out of here. But I suppress the urge to scream and calmly say, "Yes." It wasn't supposed to happen like this. I'm just supposed to walk into the office and pick up my transfer paperwork and leave. "Here's the letter I got two weeks ago. I passed the readmission exam so everything's all set. I just need my transfer paperwork."

She takes the letter and starts reading it. I wait. It takes her about five minutes to read four paragraphs. Her lips move the whole time. She finishes and hands it back to me and then shrugs. "It's not here," she says dismissively, and looks at the next student behind me. "What do you need?"

"No, wait. You said the same thing yesterday and the day before. Do you know if maybe it was already sent or faxed to Hazelhurst?"

"No, we don't do that and I'd have a record of that anyway."

"But I'm supposed to transfer to Hazelhurst Academy Monday morning."

"I'll check the computer," she says, obviously getting annoyed, but still she types in my name. The screen changes, so I guess my records come up. She shakes her head slowly. "There's nothing here as far as your records are concerned regarding a transfer. There's a transfer in from a month and a half ago. That's it."

"No, that's wrong."

"Hold on." She turns around and yells out to other staffers. "Hey, anybody have transfer paperwork on Denise Lewis?"

"No, Kenisha Lewis, my name is *Kenisha Lewis*," I reiterate.

"Make that Kenisha Lewis." She waits a half second. Nobody responds, but it wasn't like anybody was actually paying attention to what she said anyway.

She shrugs. "Are you sure you're supposed to transfer?"

"Yes. Like I said, I passed the readmission test. They said it would only take a few days. That was two weeks ago. The new grading period begins Monday. I talked to the assistant principal at the end of last week. He said he was going to contact Hazelhurst Academy and see what was going on. Do you know if he did that?"

"No. I don't see anything about that, and he's been out sick all week."

"Can you contact him and see what happened?"

"No," she says flatly.

"So what do I do then?" I ask.

She shrugs and looks at the student behind me and nods. "Next!"

I guess I got my answer.

CHAPTER 2

Down Another Rabbit Hole

"The ending in a fairy tale is almost the same thing as waking up from a nightmare. They both seem real at the time. But when you look closer you see the cracks in reality."

—*Facebook.com*

NOW *what?*

I'm standing here trying to figure out what just happened. Okay, I'm not stupid. I wasn't born yesterday. I'm sixteen years old, smart, focused and can take care of myself—mostly. I live with my grandmother and sometimes with my dad. But all that is to say that I'm no fool. I have a good head on my shoulders. Okay, maybe I had some problems before, but all that's over with now. See, back then, I trusted the wrong people and almost got myself jammed up. I messed up. I admit it. But I'm fine now. Well, not really. The thing is I'm not where I'm supposed to be. I was supposed to be out of Penn Hall five days ago.

So being pissed is an understatement. I storm out of the administrative office and head down the hall to my locker.

Seriously, this can't be happening. Every time I try to get my life back together, something happens to get in my way. I know I did everything I was supposed to do. I studied, I passed the stupid test and I got the readmission letter. Something had to have happened after that. I gotta figure out what. My dad—I need to find him. He was supposed to write Hazelhurst Academy a check last week. As far as I can figure, that's the only thing holding everything up. I need to make sure he did what he was supposed to do. I pull out my cell and send him a text message.

I don't really expect an answer. I called him three times this week and texted him like twice every day. He's been MIA. Okay, I get it. I know my dad's been distracted lately. It's the whole new family thing that gets him all *weirded* out. I guess a new baby in the house can do that. And I know dealing with Courtney, my dad's live-in whatever, and her crazy-ass self can do that, too. Now that she's dealing with that postpartum thing it must really be a hot mess.

I went over there last weekend, but only stayed one night. Courtney was screaming her head off. The thing is, she's usually screaming her head off about something. But last weekend she was unreal, even by her standards. She kept yelling about wanting my dad to marry her and swearing if he didn't she'd never speak to him again.

Really, truthfully, I don't think that was much of a threat. Knowing my dad, Courtney not speaking to him was probably exactly what he wanted. Then of course, seeing his expression as he ran out of the house more than proved the point. I didn't see him the rest of the night. That didn't stop Courtney from still losing her mind.

The boys, Kenneth James Jr., named after my dad, and Jason, my other half brother, stayed by my side the whole time I was there. They even slept in my bedroom. They fell asleep on my bed watching *Monsters, Inc.* I didn't have the heart to move them to their bedroom. I felt bad for them. When I was leaving, they cried and wanted to come with me. Courtney was pissed, and my dad was MIA as usual. It's a trick he perfected years ago. When there's drama, he disappears. So Saturday afternoon I left.

"Kenisha."

I turn around to see Ms. Grayson standing in the hall. I must have blown right past her without even seeing her. "I gotta go, Ms. Grayson," I say, before she adds more drama to my day.

"What's going on with you?"

"I'm fine," I say, and start walking again.

"Hold up. Whatever it is you have to do can wait a few minutes." She walks over to me with her eyebrows all scrunched together frowning. "Now, what's going on with you lately? A month ago you were my best student. Now you're surly, angry and ambivalent. Your grades are all over the board lately. You're not focusing. Are you having family problems?" she asks.

I start laughing. "Me, family problems—you gotta be kidding, right? Which ones?" I ask sarcastically. She looks at me. I hate having to explain. "Okay, you mean the family problem where my dad kicked me and my mom out of our Virginia house a few months ago, so he could move his pregnant girlfriend in. Or maybe you're talking about the one where my mom took a handful of pills and killed herself. Oh, and then there's some drug dealing nut–job in the neighborhood who tried to rape me two weeks ago. So exactly which family drama are you talking about?"

She looks stunned. "Kenisha, I'm so sorry," she whispers.

"Well don't be. Like I said before, I'm fine."

"No, you're not. Come on. Let's go back to the classroom and talk. We can figure some of this out."

"I can't. I have to go home and take care of something, then everything will be fine after that." I start walking away.

"Kenisha, wait."

"I gotta go, Ms. Grayson."

"All right, Kenisha, but I want to talk to you first thing Monday morning. I get in early and I don't have a first period class. Just tell your teacher to call me and I'll excuse you from the class."

"Yeah, okay," I say, knowing as soon as I talk to my dad, that isn't going to happen. So I hurry to my locker but know I'm already too late 'cause I can hear them before I even turn the corner. Troy and his boys are at his locker, which is right next to mine. Crap, more drama. This is the last thing I need. I'm so not in the mood for him. I start walking toward my locker, ignoring him as his boys back up smiling. Troy turns around. He sees me. Shit. Here we go.

"Hey, it's Kenishiwa. You waiting around for me," he says.

I roll my eyes and just keep walking. I'm so not in the mood for this right now. The thing is I know he's kind of seeing Sierra, so why he's always up in my face is beyond me. Troy Carson is one of the most popular guys in school. That's mostly because he plays football and runs track. He's in the eleventh grade, same as me, and already he has college teams checkin' him. Most of the girls think he's cute and some admitted to already sleeping with him just for the props. They'd probably cut off a limb to have their locker next to his. Me, I could care less. He's loud and obnoxious and thinks he's the shit.

Right now he leans back against my locker and smiles at me. I walk over and glare at him. "Excuse me," I say, knowing it isn't going to be that easy.

His eyes are real dark brown, and they do this twinkle thing. His skin is milk chocolate and smooth like silk. He's tall with wide shoulders and thick biceps. He dresses nice, really nice, and I hear his family has deep pockets. He has nice hair that he keeps cut short, and he wears a small earring in each earlobe. Okay, fine, I admit it. He's cute and all, but he's still an asshole.

His smile widens as he slowly moves to the side, allowing me to get to my locker. But he's still too close. He leans down and talks loud enough for his boys to hear. "So, Kenishiwa, what you doin' this weekend? I know your boy D's not around anymore and everybody knows he was tappin' that on the regular, so why don't you come over to my place? You and me can hang out."

"What?"

"You heard me. Don't act like you don't know. I can give you what you need now that your boy's not around." His friends start laughing, slapping hands and bumping fists.

I sigh heavily, then spin my combination and open my locker. I know I just have to ignore him. I pivot my shoulder, and the door swings wider almost clipping his face. He jerks back quickly. His boys start laughing again, but I ignore them, too. I grab my jacket and then everything else except for the school books that I need to turn back in. It's mostly empty anyway 'cause I thought I was leaving today.

Troy leans against another locker looking directly at me. He keeps talking, spouting off his usual crap about going out with him. His boys, a brainless bunch of football jocks, look on laughing moronically. It's like every stupid typical high school scene from every stupid typical high school movie ever made. It's so old and tired. Seriously, can he really be this dumb? I can imagine in another ten years, he'll be the guy who gets slapped with a sexual harassment lawsuit and considers it business as usual. But whatever, I just keep grabbing my stuff and say nothing.

"So what, you ain't talking now?"

"Please, talking to you is an exercise in futility."

"What?" he says, apparently clueless. Seeing his expression, it hits me. He probably doesn't know what I just said. His boys, standing behind him, start laughing *at* him instead of *with* him.

He glares at me. His expression is completely blank, and he's speechless. It occurs to me that saying something so obviously sarcastic might have whiplashed his brain. Still, Troy Carson speechless. I kinda like the sound of that. All of a sudden I'm feeling much better, so I keep going. "For real, your ego is unbelievable. Exactly what fragments of your tiny cerebrum have disconnected from your vocal cords?"

"What did you just say to me?" he mumbles, obviously trying to figure out what I said. See, in this school, girls aren't supposed to talk to him like this. He's Troy Carson, football player, quarterback and the *shit*. We're just supposed to jump when he says so and be happy about it. Not.

"You heard exactly what I said." I'm smiling as I close my locker. "Tell you what, when you figure out what that means, get back to me." Of course now I'm lovin' this 'cause his boys are really laughing at him now even though they don't have a clue, either. I look at them. They are all cracking up except one, Boyce. I don't know his last name. He's not the type of person you want to know all that well. He's a stone-cold thug with serious lockdown issues. Everything about him pointed to an ending involving a needle in the arm or a bullet in the head. It was just a matter of time for either or both.

"Come on, man, screw her stuck-up ass. We ain't got time for this shit. We got stuff to do," Boyce says anxiously.

"Nah, nah, I want to hear this," Troy begins playfully.

"You's a stupid ass, why you kissing up behind her, man?"

"What?"

"You don't need her shit. Let's go."

"Yo, man, can you hold up a minute?" Troy says. The other guys are deathly quiet. No one seems to even be breathing.

"Yo, screw this and screw this schoolgirl shit."

Troy turns to him, and the rest of his crew seem to take a

step back. Nobody says a word and I just stand there, 'cause it is obvious something is about to jump off since Boyce had stepped up to Troy. "Let's go, man," Boyce reiterates forcefully.

Troy doesn't say anything to him this time. He just turns back to me. "A'ight this time—frontin' with jokes just 'cause you think you know two big words."

"That's two more than you know," I say, as I start walking away. I had enough of this game. Unfortunately, I have to walk past his friends to get to my exit. Boyce glares at me as I pass him. I swear he looked like pure evil. I looked away. Hell, I wasn't crazy.

"Bitch," Troy says, loud enough for me to hear.

"Takes one to know one, bitch," I whisper under my breath louder than I thought. His boys hear me and start laughing at him again.

"What did you say?" he asks quickly.

"That's an excellent question, Mr. Carson. Exactly what did you just say?"

Everybody turns and sees Ms. Grayson approaching. Troy doesn't turn. Instead he's looking right at me. His eyes are really dark as he glares. I know he's pissed, but right now I don't really care. Ms. Grayson pulls him to the side. His boys start walking away slowly.

I walk away, knowing he'd have a headache the rest of the day. Ms. Grayson is talking to him about having respect. He said something, blaming me, but I didn't hear it. I start laughing anyway. Okay, I admit it. That was fun. Messing with Troy's head was like playing with my little brothers.

The only difference is they're not yet five. Still, mentally there's not a lot of difference.

So I get to the end of the hall nearest my exit and see my ex-friend Cassie. She's sitting on the bench at the exit. We used to meet up like this all the time and walk home together. She stands when I approach. I shake my head and roll my eyes. I know this bitch isn't about to try and talk to me after everything she did.

"Kenisha, can we talk?" she says quietly.

I have nothing to say to her. Still don't, so I just keep walking. I don't even bother saying, *"hell, no."*

"Kenisha. Kenisha. Kenisha."

She keeps calling me, so I finally stop and stare at her like she's crazy. I can't believe she has the nerve to try and talk to me after what she did. Like I'm not supposed to re-member she caused all this drama in the first place. Having somebody stab me in the back once is all the lesson I need to learn. I don't trust her, and she knows it. So how am I supposed to be friends with someone I don't trust? I don't know what she thinks she's doing, or what she's up to, but whatever.

She hurries and stands in front of me, blocking my way. "Kenisha, I know you're mad at me. But for real, it wasn't my fault. Whatever happened, I don't remember most of it. I swear. It was Darien. He gave me something. He made me do it. I didn't want to call you like that. But I was scared of him. He said he was gonna cut me if I didn't call you. I didn't know what to do. I didn't know what was gonna happen. I swear I didn't."

I don't say anything to her. I just start walking again.

She's still playing all innocent. She does that all the time. Nobody knows what she's really like, but I do. I saw it in her eyes that night. At least with my used-to-be friend Chili Rodriguez, we all knew she was a hater. But Cassie is undercover with her stuff.

"Kenisha, wait, it wasn't my fault. It was Darien."

"Look, Cassie," I finally say, breaking my long silence with her, "I'm done with all that mess. I don't really care."

"So can't we be friends again?" she asks quietly.

I just look at her thinking about everything she did to set me up. "You called me on the phone. You lied and told me Ursula needed my help. Then when I went over there, you ran out and left me alone with crazy-ass Darien. *Friends!* Please, do you really need me to answer that question?" To her credit, she looked almost horrified at hearing what I'd said. Like she didn't know, *please*.

"Kenisha, I'm sorry. I was scared and Darien gave me something. I didn't know what he was gonna do, I swear."

"Whatever. Like I said, I'm done with all that drama." I move around her to walk away.

"But, wait. I know you're still mad at me, but I just wanted to warn you that he knows about the stuff you took from him."

"What stuff I took? I didn't take anything from him."

"He thinks you did, from his room that night."

"I don't know what game he's playing, but I didn't take anything from his room. Why would I? I don't need or want anything from him."

She shrugs. "That's just what I heard," she says.

Okay, this is more drama that I don't need to be dealing with right now. Darien was locked up and that's all I care about. "Whatever," I say and start walking again. So a minute later I get outside and see that it's been drizzling. It's not enough to soak everything but just enough to be messy. I pull my hoodie up, put my earbuds in but decide not to turn my music on just yet. I adjust my backpack on my shoulder, then start walking. Mostly everybody else takes a school bus and they're all gone, but since I only live a few blocks away, I walk.

Darien, Cassie, Troy, forget all that. I need to focus and try to figure out what happened to my transfer papers. But also, there's a tingling feeling in the back of my mind thinking that it was all some big joke on me. Like it never happened, like I never passed the readmission test, and the letter was just a mistake.

I walk home alone and it's okay with me. It gives me time to think. The last thing I need are more pretend friends like Cassie and Chili. I have for-real friends, Jalisa and Diamond, and that's enough for me. So, I'm walking and trying to figure out what happened, then I hear somebody calling my name. I keep walking like I don't hear anything, but it's kinda hard not to. They're screaming my name across the parking lot. I seriously don't want to be bothered right now.

CHAPTER 3

From Bad to Worse, to Even Worse

"It seems like every time I turn around, something else happens to me that's not my fault. For real, right now I feel like I have a giant bull's-eye on my back and everybody's taking aim. It's not me being paranoid. It's for real."

—MySpace.com

"kenisha. Hey, Kenisha, wait up, Kenisha. You hear me, girl."

"Crap," I mutter under my breath. I know the voice. It's Jerome Tyler, Li'l T to mostly everybody. He's a tall and lean freshman with dreams of playing in the big leagues. He lives around the way and is always into something. He's also the biggest gossip in the neighborhood. If you need information on anything going on, he's the guy to talk to. I have no idea how he knows everybody's business, but he does.

He calls my name again. I seriously don't feel like stopping and talking. All I'm thinking about is getting home, finding my dad, straightening this mess out and chilling. So

I keep walking. Li'l T comes running up beside me. "Hey, girl, you heard me calling you. What, you acting like you don't know nobody now?"

I look over at him and pull my earbuds pretending like I really didn't hear him calling my name. "Oh, hey, Jerome," I say drily, calling him by his real name, hoping that's gonna annoy him enough to keep going. It doesn't. You can always depend on Li'l T not to take a hint. Anyway, he stops right beside me and starts talking about what happened this morning with the fight. He was right there and saw everything, big surprise. His friends trail behind listening close. I really am not paying attention. I already heard most of this already anyway.

"So, what you up to this weekend?" he asks.

"Nothing," I say, figuring I'd be getting my stuff together to transfer schools. I knew I wouldn't have much time for anything else.

"A'ight, be like that. You gonna need a brotha one day."

I guess he finally caught the dryness in my tone. "For real, nothing," I said more forcibly. "There's nothing going on this weekend. I'll probably go to Virginia and hang with my girls."

"See, now that's what I'm talkin' 'bout. So, when you gonna hook a brotha up with Diamond like you promised?" he asks. I laugh out loud. The image of my friend Diamond with Li'l T is too absurd. You just don't even know. "What's so funny?" he asks, as if he didn't know.

"Jerome, please, you know that's not even about to happen."

"See, now you blocking on me. I see the way Diamond be checkin' a brotha out. She likes what she sees. She knows what I got to offer."

Li'l T is a dreamer. At one time he wanted to hook up with me, my girl Jalisa and then with my ex-friend Chili. Not to mention a few others after that. "Not gonna happen," I repeat.

"Why not?" he asks, only half serious.

"First of all, I never promised I'd hook you up with anybody, especially one of my girls. And secondly, you know Diamond is way too old for you. And she's seriously way out of your league."

"What you talkin' 'bout?"

"I'm talking about the fact that you can't speak a full sentence in proper English, even if your life depended on it. You know Diamond doesn't play that. Besides, she's kind of seeing someone now."

"Seeing somebody," he says indignantly. "Who she seeing?"

"Not you," I say, teasingly. His friends start laughing.

"Yeah, yeah, whatever, you know Diamond's got a thing for me," he boasts. I give him the in-your-dreams look. He understands and laughs, too. "A'ight, a'ight," he says half laughing. We keep walking. Then when we are right around the corner from my house he looks back, seeing that his friends have stopped to talk to someone. "Umm, listen, I hear D might be getting out in a minute," he says, quietly.

I almost stumble as I turn and look at him. The black eye I'd given him by accident was just about gone, but you could still see the shadow of where I punched him. Of course, nearly everybody else seems to think D gave it to him. One guess as to how that rumor got started.

"Where'd you hear that?" I ask, hoping he was wrong, but knowing better. Anyone else, I would have seriously challenged the information, but not Li'l T. He knew what he knew and that was it. Besides, I knew Darien's father had major pull when it came to things like that. This wasn't the first time he got off easy.

"I heard it," he says. I could hear the tenseness in his voice and see his strained blank expression as he stared straight ahead. "You scared?" he asks, finally turning to me.

"No," I lie.

"Yeah, me neither," he says.

I know he's lying, just like he knows I was, too. I don't blame him. Hearing that Darien was getting out nearly stopped my heart. I don't know what I'd do if I actually ran into him again. The last time I saw him, the paramedics were putting him into an ambulance. Thanks to me, he had a broken arm, and Terrence had messed his face up big-time. He had turned and looked at me after he got inside the ambulance. Even now I can feel the icy chill and viciousness behind his vengeful stare. I was still thinking about that night when Li'l T asked me something. I didn't hear him. "Huh, what?" I say.

"I asked if you're going over to Gia's place tonight. You heard about her great-uncle, right?"

"No," I say, still only half listening. I was still stuck on the possibility of Darien getting out.

"He died last night."

"Who died?" I ask, more interested now.

"Mr. Russell. Oh, snap, I forgot. You don't know Gia, do you? She left before you got here this summer." Then he smiles like suddenly he has some new deep dark secret.

"Who's Gia?" I ask.

"Just a girl, never mind," he says, blowing me off.

Okay, I've known Li'l T too long not to know when he's hiding something. And for him to say *never mind* about a rumor, or anything else, and not tell me, meant it was something major. So of course I had to know what it was. "Nah, nah, you started this. Now you have to tell me. Who's Gia?" I ask again, loud enough for his boys to hear. They'd been lagging behind and then quickened their pace to hear what was going on.

"Hey, check, there's your man," Li'l T says, seeing lawn mower guy sitting on the steps in front of his house.

I look over. Terrence Butler, lawn mower guy, looks up at me as we approach. I smile. I seriously love looking at his eyes. They're light, almost hazel. He has a sweet caramel-colored complexion and long curly lashes that would make a supermodel jealous. His hair is cut short, light brown with natural blond highlights. I think his grandfather is white, but he never talks about him much. He looks the same except for the constant frown on his face when he looks at me now. That's new. I can see he's mad. I know it's because I was hanging out with Darien before, but all that's done. I told him that.

After everything happened that night, the next day he seemed fine. We talked and walked like nothing was wrong. Now it's all different again, and I don't know why. We barely talk on the phone. When I text him, the only reply I get is that he'll hit me up later. Anyway, I haven't seen him in almost two weeks.

"Hey, T," Li'l T says joyfully, "What's up, my man? How's it going?" Terrence stands, and they shake hands and bump shoulders, in that half hug guys do.

"Sup, Li'l T," Terrence says and then looks at me and frowns, then greets Li'l T's friends. "How's it going at The Penn?"

"Yeah, well, you know a brotha be handling his business," Li'l T boasts. "I'm about to go hard, man. I'm just steppin' in where you left off."

"Bet," Terrence says, then nods. Li'l T's boys nod, as well. They look like the stupid bobblehead toys my little brothers play with. I roll my eyes 'cause this conversation is totally ridiculous. It's all big bravado spiked with testosterone and BS.

So they're all laughing and talking like I'm not here and don't even exist. And I'm just standing there looking stupid. I hate when I do this. I look at Terrence, my lawn mower guy. I remember the first time I saw him. He was mowing my grandmother's lawn the day we were moving here. Later, I sat watching him putting stuff away in the shed out back. He was too cute, and I was checking him out big-time.

It was hot. He had taken his T-shirt off and had tucked it into his back pocket. His chest and back were seriously chiseled. I'm talking built with LL Cool J biceps, triceps and abs. I was staring at him like I lost my mind. But I couldn't help it. Then he turned and started watching me watch him. I was totally in la-la land, 'cause I didn't even notice.

We started talking after that and got to know each other. We'd been hanging out ever since, but that was before.

So now Li'l T and his boys are leaving and Terrence sits back down and looks up at me. He's got this seriously strange expression on his face. I don't know how to describe it. It's like he wants to say something, but doesn't.

"You're late," I say, half joking but really not. He was supposed to come home from college a week ago. He didn't. He didn't call to let me know he wasn't coming.

"Don't start," he warned, and then turned to look down the street away from me.

"I'm just saying. It would have been nice to see you last week. I missed you." He nods, but doesn't respond. I know he's still pissed about the Darien thing. I said I was sorry. I don't know what else to do.

"Look, I was busy, a'ight. I had exams and other stuff to deal with."

"How did the exams go?" I ask.

"Fine."

Neither one of us speaks for a while. We are just there, occupying space, staring in opposite directions. "How's school?" I ask, hopefully bringing up a safe subject we can both talk about and relate to.

"It's a'ight."

"How's the fraternity? Having fun?"

"It's a'ight."

I sit down beside him and put my books on my lap. I look up and down the street and then glance at him. His profile is set firm and his gaze steady. He has his head down staring at the bottom step like before when Li'l T and I first walked up. I know something's on his mind. I just wish he'd tell me what it is. So I ask. "Do you want to tell me what's going on with you?"

"What makes you think something's going on with me?"

"Because you're acting different, all mad and stiff."

"I'm not mad," he says. I suck my teeth in response, 'cause I know he's lying. "Nothing's going on," he says unconvincingly.

"You don't do that very well."

He turns and looks at me. "Do what?"

"Lie to me," I say, then stand up. "Do you want to do something tonight, hang out or something? We can go to Virginia. You said you wanted to see my new baby sister," I say.

"Nah, I gotta get back to school tonight."

"What, tonight?" I ask, surprised. "But it's Friday, there's no classes tomorrow. You just got here."

"No, I came home last night."

"Last night, why didn't you call me?"

"I was busy and it was late when I got in."

"So that's it?"

"Yeah, that's it," he said.

Okay, forget this. If he just doesn't want to do this, then that's fine with me. I know when I'm not wanted. "Fine, later," I say and stand up to walk away, then stop.

"Hey, hi, you ready?"

I turn around and look up, seeing this girl walking down the front steps of Terrence's house. She is looking right at me. I look at Terrence. He looks at her and nods. "Yeah, I'm ready," he says.

"Hi. I'm Gia. You're Kenisha, right?" she asks. I nod silently. "I used to live down the street."

"Hi," I say, cautiously, not knowing exactly who she is.

"I heard about what happened with Darien a couple of weeks ago. That must have been scary. Darien's such an ass, always has been. But I like how you beat him down with his stupid trophies. It sounded like poetic justice." She smiles, obviously amused.

"Yeah," I say stupidly. Again, it looks like everyone knew what Darien was really like, except me. I glance at Terrence who'd stood up and was looking down the street. Then it gets strange 'cause nobody is saying anything. We are all there, just standing there looking at each other.

"Umm, T, we gotta go do that thing. It was nice meeting you, Kenisha," Gia says and then walks down the steps between us. She looks at Terrence as she passes. He nods as she starts walking down the street.

"Yeah, later," he says with a nod, and then he turns and follows her.

It wasn't what she said or what he said. It was just something in the air between them, that all of a sudden made it really clear to me. There was definitely something I didn't know. So, I guess that was it. It's obvious that he is still blaming me because he had to go to the police station that night. Yeah, I get it. It was my fault. I shouldn't have been where I was, and he was protecting me and got all caught up in my drama, but everything turned out fine, except he's still mad and now there's a Gia.

I watch them walk away and hope he turns around. He does. He half smiles. I do, too. I don't know what it means. I hope it means something good. I really miss my lawn mower guy.

I start walking the other way to my grandmother's house. I can't believe my day. I have no transfer papers to go to Hazelhurst on Monday. Darien and his crazy-ass might be getting out of lockup. Terrence is stuck on acting stupid around me. And now, there's a Gia. TGIF?

CHAPTER 4

Just Leave Me Alone

"The definition of water torture is the incessant dripping of water on the forehead. That's how I feel, slowly, continuously, forever, dripping drama. Need I say more?"

—Facebook.com

SO I head up my grandmother's front steps and get to the small porch. I turn around and see Terrence and Gia walking farther down the street together. I can hear her laughing. She pushes at him playfully. At least they're not all hugged up. But they're talking, like we used to. WTF. Whatever. I unlock the front door and go inside. My day is already trashed. I seriously don't need any more drama.

As soon as I walk in I can tell my grandmother is in the kitchen baking. The whole house is lit up and smelling just like a slice of heaven. I drop my books and jacket on the stairs and head straight to the kitchen. I stand in the doorway watching her pull a Bundt cake out of the oven. My stomach growls so loud I know she had to hear me. "Umm,

I hope that's for us, 'cause I'm starved," I say, eyeing the big fat slice I want as soon as it cools off.

"Good afternoon," my grandmother says, always reminding me of my manners.

"Sorry. Hi, Grandmom," I say automatically. She's such a trip. She's small, petite, with silver-gray hair and an always-knowing smile. She has a way of looking at a person and knowing everything there is to know. At least that's how I see it. She looks just like what I guess my mom would have looked like had she lived to old age.

"Is that for us? Please, please tell me that's for us." My grandmother is forever baking cakes or making potato salad, a ham or frying chicken for somebody else. Whenever there's a problem in the neighborhood, you can tell because she's cooking something for somebody. I hover close as she sits the hot cake pan on a wire rack. The aroma is incredible.

"No. It's for the family down the street. I don't know if you know them—Charlotte Russell."

"I know Ms. Lottie."

She nods. "Charlotte's brother passed last night. He's been sick for a while."

"Oh, I'm sorry to hear that. Did you know him?"

"Lord, yes, Laurence and I go way back. We went to school together. He was a good man. He was kind and considerate. No matter what, he always had a pleasant word to say. Just seeing him sometimes would brighten my day."

"I'm sorry," I say, not knowing exactly why I should be.

She starts talking again. This time about how she remembered him years ago when they were young together. She goes on and on. Stories like this just lose me. So I really am not paying much attention. I have my eye on the cake again. Then she says something about marriage. "Wait, so he was like your serious boyfriend a long time ago?"

She smiles and nods. "Yes, a very, very long time ago. He was much older than I was and it was way before I knew your grandfather."

It was weird. I can't seem to imagine my grandmother having a boyfriend. "How close were you two?"

"Very close," she says.

I look at her. It wasn't so much what she said, but how she said it. I got the feeling they were more than just friends. "Did my grandfather know about him?"

"Oh, yes, he knew," she says, then laughs. "He hated the fact that we were still friends even after everything that happened."

"What do you mean even after everything?"

She turns and looks at me. "What, do you think you're the only one who's had drama in their life? Missy, I know drama. I know drama very well."

Okay, this is just getting weird. It is sounding more and more like a love triangle to me. The oven timer sounds and I hurry to stop it. I want to get back to the conversation we were having. "What kind of drama?" I ask.

She laughs again. "You young people think you invented the concept of drama. Lord knows I had some twisting in my day. But that's a story for another time. Right now I need to get myself out of here and get this cake delivered."

I couldn't believe she'd open the door and then just drop it like that. "Grandmom, you can't just leave me hanging."

"Use a toothpick, check the cake and see if it's done."

I open the oven door. The smell of lemon vanilla hits me in a hot flash in my face. I lean back, but I can still see a smaller pound cake in the oven. I love it when my grandmother cooks lemon pound cake. I grab a toothpick and stick it in the center. It comes out clean. The cake's done. I grab oven mitts and take it out and sit it on the other wire rack on the table.

"Man, this smells so good." My nose is practically on top of the cake. Lemon and vanilla, there's nothing like it.

"That one's for you." She nods.

I smile. Damn, this made my day. "Thanks, Grandmom. This is the first good thing to happen all day." I give her a hug, and I surprise myself, 'cause I have a hard time letting go. I just hold on to her.

"Had a bad one, huh, baby?" she asks, gently patting my back.

I nod. Suddenly the thought of everything begins to weigh down on me—no transfer papers, Darien maybe getting out and now Gia. "Yeah, something like that," I say, pulling a chair out.

She stops what she's doing and turns to me. "What happened?"

I sit heavily. "I went to the school office again today. My transfer papers weren't there again. The woman behind the desk said to check back Monday morning. They've been telling me that all week."

"All week?" she says, surprised. "Why didn't you tell me?"

My grandmother sits down and holds my hand as she

takes a deep breath. I look at her face. Her eyes are soft and caring. She knows how much I want to go back to Hazelhurst. "I'm sorry, sweetie," she says quietly. "Well, first thing Monday morning I'm going up there to see what's going on."

"I'm gonna call my dad again. He was supposed to send Hazelhurst a check for my tuition. I guess he forgot with everything going on with the baby and all. I'm hoping that's the only holdup."

"I'm sure that's all it is," she says, much less reassuring than I expected. She immediately starts drizzling the sweet glaze on top of the cake.

"Yeah, I guess so," I say. Then I look at her expression as she works. She looks like she is concentrating, but I can see there is something else. I can't tell if she meant what she said or not. I'm thinking not. My dad has never been one of her favorite people, but she put up with him—first because of my mom and now because of me. "I'm a go change my clothes," I say, then stand up and look around the kitchen before heading out.

"Are you going for your run?" she asks.

I think about it a few seconds. For the last two weeks I've run after school. It calms me down, but I really don't feel like it today. "Nah, not today, I'll go tomorrow morning," I say. She nods.

"Oh, I almost forgot, you received a few phone calls today," she says.

"Huh? Me?" I ask awkwardly, knowing that nobody I know even had my grandmother's home number. She looks at me sternly expecting a better reply. "I mean, that's weird 'cause nobody knows your number."

"Apparently someone does. One caller was a young man, the other was a girl's voice. Neither wanted to leave their name or a phone number. They both said they'd call you back later this evening."

I nod. It was weird though. I didn't think anybody knew my grandmother's home number. But I guess somebody does. Hell, even I have to look it up on my cell. "Grandmom, I'm going to go up and change. I'm meeting Jalisa and Diamond at the dance studio tonight. We'll probably go to the Pizza Place after that."

"That's fine. I'll be at Charlotte's most of the evening."

"Okay." I leave the kitchen, grab my stuff off the step, then go upstairs to my room. I start to charge my cell, then see Darien's broken-ass trophy on the floor almost under my bed. I smile. It was my trophy now. It was the biggest one from that night in his bedroom. I don't know why I didn't just give it back to Ursula, but I didn't. I kept it. Seeing it always made me feel good. I found it the next morning after everything happened. I must have dropped it on the front porch when I was trying to open the door that night. But right now, seeing it sitting there, and knowing Darien might get out, was making me sick. I pick it up and put it behind the door, out of sight, out of mind.

I wash up and change my clothes. I am packing my dance bag when my cell rings. I check the caller ID. It's Jalisa. I pick up. "Hey, girl," I say happily. It is always good to hear from my girls.

"Hey, you ready? We're almost there."

"Yeah, give me a minute."

"Too late, we're here."

"What?" I ask. There is a knock on my bedroom door, then giggling and laughter outside. I open my bedroom door to see my girls standing there smiling and laughing. It is so good to see them. I just start laughing, too.

"Hey," Diamond says, as we hug. "Your grandmom let us in. She said to tell you she's on her way out and to not get in any trouble tonight."

"Yeah, like that's gonna happen," Jalisa jokes, as we hug, too. "Girl, you stay knee-deep in drama twenty-four-seven."

"Excuse me, but I do not get in trouble," I say. "Much."

Diamond and Jalisa look at each other and then at me and break up laughing. I have to laugh, too. "Man, I can't wait for Monday. It's gonna be so perfect having you back at school again," Jalisa says.

"I know, right," Diamond adds happily. "Watch out, Hazelhurst Academy, the girls are back in town." They laugh, then see I'm not smiling.

"What's wrong?" Jalisa asks.

"My transfer papers weren't at Penn today. They don't know anything about me going to Hazelhurst on Monday."

"But you passed the exam," Diamond says.

"Yeah, you aced it. What else do they want?" Jalisa adds.

"I don't know. I need to talk to my dad and make sure he paid the tuition on time. You know how they get about money. Anyway, that's the only thing I can think of holding it up."

"A'ight, that's cool then. You just have to pay when you get there on Monday morning."

"Ah, man, I can't wait to see Chili's face when you walk your ass back into class." We start laughing again. "She's such a joke. She's got this little stomach and she walks around poking it out wanting everyone to see that she's pregnant."

"Yeah, and now everybody's saying that it's not even LaVon's baby. They're talking about her being with some college basketball player," Diamond says.

"I heard that. I also heard he was married," Jalisa adds.

"Seriously, I can believe it," I say.

"Chili is such a skank and a liar."

"She'll say anything to get what she wants."

"And right now she wants LaVon, my sloppy seconds." We laugh for a while this time.

"Okay, come on now. I feel like dancing."

"Yeah, me, too."

"Me, three."

Diamond and Jalisa head to the stairs. When I go the other way, they turn to look at me. "Where are you going?"

"Downstairs," I say. They look at me strangely. "Want to see something cool? Come on, check this out." They come back and follow me to the closet door. I open it and they see boxes and linens.

"It's a closet," Jalisa says. I push the shelving on the side and it easily slides over. There is a small landing and stairs. "Oh, cool, check this out, stairs," Jalisa adds.

"I didn't know you had a back staircase," Diamond says.

"Not a lot of people do."

"Did it come with the house?"

"I guess. My grandmother was born in this house and even her grandmother was born here. It kinda gets passed down through the generations. She told me it was once owned by these abolitionists and they hid escaped slaves. So when the hunters searched the house, the runaways would either hide in here or run down and out the back door."

"That is so cool," Diamond says.

"I know, right," Jalisa adds.

"Where do they lead?" Diamond asks.

"Duh, Diamond, downstairs," Jalisa says. "Come on, let's go down."

"Nah, I just wanted to show you. I hate going down these stairs when the pantry light's not on. It's too dark and spooky."

"Oh, come on, it's cool." Jalisa has already started down. "It's not bad. It's stairs. Just keep walking."

Diamond follows her and I go last. Seriously, I hate these stairs. I close the closet door and push the shelves and follow. Jalisa and Diamond laugh and talk the whole time. At least that makes me feel better. "Where's the light switch?" Jalisa calls up to me. I hear her voice, but we are in complete darkness.

"To the left, by the door. Hold your hand out and just keep straight. You'll bump right into it," I say. But I know there is no way she'll find the pantry door. Then all of a sudden, the door opens and the lights go on. I blink and look around. I am still near the second floor while Jalisa and Diamond are already down in the pantry.

"Oh, my God, that was so cool," Jalisa says.

"I know. If I had these, I'd never use the front stairs."

I finally get to the bottom. "I really hate those stairs."

They laugh as we go into the kitchen. We grab some water bottles and walk down the hall to the foyer. Then they stand on the front porch as I lock the deadbolt on the front door. Outside I see Terrence walking up his steps to his porch. He waves and speaks to Jalisa and Diamond. We look at each other. He nods. I do, too. That's it and nobody says anything.

We pile in Diamond's mother's small car and she drives us to the dance studio even though my grandmother lives just a couple of blocks away. She parks and we walk into Freeman like we own it. But for real, this is our place. This is where we met when we were four years old. They still have pictures of us on the walls. Mostly everybody knows us here. The young kids all look up to us. We dance tap, ballet, jazz and modern, but our favorite, of course, is hip-hop. We say hi to some dance instructors, then go upstairs to the private studios. That's where the advanced students go. We don't actually have class anymore, we just do our thing and practice hard.

We change out of our street sneakers and start dancing. The music's rhythm goes hard. It energizes us. We dance our routine, something we've been working on for a few weeks. When it's good enough, we're gonna show it to Gayle Harmon for one of the dance videos she choreographs. So we dance and play around and try out some new stuff Diamond came up with. Jalisa and I both add on to it. It's really starting to look good. Seriously, it's really hot.

Some dance instructors from downstairs come up to see us, including Ms. Jay, the studio manager.

They are cheering and applauding by the time we really get into it. I had gotten my sister's fiancé, Tyrece Grant, to do the music, so it was dope. We are all three doing the same step, but to a different downbeat, with different timing and different dance styles. I have on my dance sneakers, Diamond has on ballet slippers, and Jalisa has on her tap shoes. We are hot. When the music ends we have like half the school upstairs in the studio with us. They are applauding and cheering. I usually don't like the whole in-front-of-a-crowd, audience-recital thing, but this time I really like the attention. It feels great.

So we leave about two hours later. It's dark outside now, and I'm happy Diamond drove her car. We decide to stop at Giorgio's Pizza Place before going home. We eat a slice and then share a cookie like we always do. "Okay, enough of this. So, you gonna say something or what?" Jalisa asks me all of a sudden. Diamond and I look at her. I have no idea what she's talking about and apparently neither does Diamond.

"Say something about what?" I ask her.

"Please, girl, don't be acting like we didn't see all that before," she says.

Okay, I'm not fakin'. I look at her completely stumped. I swear, I have no idea what she's talking about.

"What's up with you and lawn mower guy?" Jalisa asks.

"Jalisa," Diamond says, hitting her arm.

"What, I'm just asking—it's not like we didn't see that."

I shrug. "Nah, it's okay. To tell you the truth, I don't really know what's up with him. He's acting all strange now. Maybe it's school drama, I don't know."

"Is it because of that jerk Darien?" Diamond asks quietly.

"Darien?" I ask. She nods tentatively. I shrug again. "I don't know, maybe. But he was okay with everything right after it happened. The next morning we were out walking and talking. Now all of a sudden he's all mad at me. I don't know." I shrug again.

"Can't you get him to talk about it?" Jalisa asks.

"Yeah, maybe talking will help," Diamond adds.

"I keep asking him, but he won't talk. He keeps saying everything's fine, when I know it's not. It's just messed up. I know he's got something going on."

"Guys are weird anyway," Jalisa says, looking at Diamond. I look at both of them, knowing something is up. They know I am gonna ask, so Jalisa says it before I do. "I broke up with Isaac the other day. He was trippin', acting all jealous like he owns me or something."

"He hit her," Diamond says.

"He did what?" I say, too loud and completely shocked. The insides of me start shaking. This is scary. I've been around abusers before. My mom was a hitter. She'd slap someone in a hot minute. Then Darien was a bully, and I knew, given the opportunity, he'd try something stupid. What he tried to do was beyond abuse. But I never knew a girl who actually got hit by a guy before.

"He hit me," Jalisa says.

"Oh, my God, Jalisa, are you okay?" I ask quickly. "Did he ever hit you before?"

She nods. "Yeah, he did it before. But not hit me. He got mad once and pushed me and then another time he grabbed my arm really tight and left a mark. But I didn't say anything to anybody, 'cause I thought it was my fault." She looks away. Diamond grabs and holds her hand. It is obvious she already knew about all this.

"When did this happen?" I ask.

"A couple of weeks ago," Jalisa says.

"Why didn't you tell me?" I ask both of them. They don't say anything at first. All of a sudden I am feeling completely left out. Jalisa needed me and nobody said a word. They look at each other, so I ask again. "Why didn't you tell me?" I insist.

"We didn't say anything to you 'cause you were trippin'. It was right after that party we went to at your friend's house down the street, remember. You were hanging out and partying with that Darien guy, so I didn't want to say anything to you. But it's all right now. Everything's copasetic. I told Isaac I didn't want to see him anymore."

"I'm sorry, Jalisa," I say sorrowfully. They were right. I was into my own thing and believing what Darien was telling me. "After you told him, what did he say?" I ask, starting to feel really bad that I wasn't there for my friend.

"Nothing. What could he say? He was like, 'whatever.' He told me I was a tease 'cause I wouldn't have sex with him. You know what, I'm glad I didn't 'cause he's an asshole.

He stopped speaking. Big deal, what a joke, I can't believe I was actually into him like that."

"Forget him," Diamond says. I nod in agreement.

After that we don't say much more about it. We get started talking about surface things, school, homework, music, clothes and things like that. I'm listening to Jalisa and Diamond, but still wondering about Terrence and what Isaac did to Jalisa. We're just about to leave when I see Ursula walk in. I reintroduce her to Jalisa and Diamond, even though they already met at the party she had at her house last month. We all start talking. "So, what are you doing here this late?" I ask her.

"Picking up my paycheck," she says.

"You work here?" I ask surprised, 'cause I don't remember seeing her here before.

"Yeah, I just got the job a few weeks ago. I usually work weekends. Sierra hooked me up. I think they still need somebody if you're interested."

"Nah, I'll pass," I say. Seriously, the last thing I want to be doing is smelling like somebody's pizza every weekend.

"You should try it. It's not that bad. Actually, it's pretty cool," Ursula says.

"I'll think about it," I say, knowing damn well I have no intention of working in somebody's stinky pizza place.

"A'ight, take care," she says.

"You need a ride home?" Diamond asks Ursula.

"Nah, thanks anyway. Sierra's meeting me."

"Okay, see you later," I say. Then we head out. Diamond drops me off at my grandmother's house.

"Are you staying at your dad's house this weekend?"

"Yeah, I need to talk to him about school. I think he's avoiding me, so that means I need to camp out at the house until he comes home."

"You want to go over there tonight?"

"Nah, a friend of my grandmother's just died. I was gonna hang around here and then head over to my dad's tomorrow. I'm a go to his office first. He's usually there hiding from Courtney Saturday mornings." I get out of the car.

"A'ight, we're hanging at the mall tomorrow night."

"Cool, I'll see ya'll there," I say. I hurry up the steps to the porch as they drive away. I stay outside a few minutes watching until I see the red taillight turn the corner. I turn around and look at Terrence's porch. There's nobody outside and his car is gone. I decide to text him. No surprise, he doesn't answer, so I just go inside.

As soon as I do I stop 'cause something seems different. I don't know what it is, but something's off. I look around the living room and dining room, then go into the kitchen. The first thing I see is the back door open. I know that is wrong. My grandmother always locks the house up when she goes out. But she did look troubled before, so maybe she forgot. I walk to the open door and look outside. There is no one around, so I close and lock the door.

It's around ten-thirty. My grandmother isn't home yet, so I just go to my room. I get on Facebook and write on some of my friends' walls. Then I hit MySpace and post about dancing. Afterward, I tweet a quick update and then email my sister, Jade. She is online, so we IM for about ten minutes.

I go downstairs to get a piece of cake. Then I stop in the

living room to turn the lights on, knowing that my grandmother will be in soon. As I head back upstairs, I hear the key in the latch and turn around. She walks in the door. I don't think she saw me. She looks tired and weary. "Hi, Grandmom. You okay?"

She looks up, seeing me on the steps. She smiles. "Kenisha, I thought you'd still be out with your friends, or in Virginia."

"Nah, I didn't feel like hanging out late. How was your night?" I ask. It's a stupid question, I know, but still it seems okay to ask. "How's Ms. Lottie?"

"She's all broken up, poor baby. Thank God her granddaughter came home to be with her. I don't know what she would have done if she hadn't. Gia is such a sweet girl."

Gia? I look up. That damn name has been popping in my world all day. "Who's Gia?" I ask my grandmother, knowing she'll tell me something.

"Gia Henderson used to come stay the summers with her grandmother. Her parents live somewhere outside of Baltimore now. They used to live in Atlanta I think. She's a sweet girl like her mother. We had a nice talk this evening. She goes to Howard, you know. This is her second year."

"You talked with her?"

"Yes, of course. She's staying with her grandmother for the next few days. She'll be a comfort. Charlotte is taking her brother's passing pretty hard."

"I think I'll go over tomorrow," I say.

My grandmother looks at me and smiles warmly. "That would be nice. I'm sure she'll appreciate that."

"Okay," I say, acting like I'm all right with all this. I don't think I really am. The thing is, I don't know this Gia, and just meeting her today like that wasn't all that cool. It was obvious she and Terrence had something. I don't know what it was or is, but it's something. "Can I get you something, Grandmom?"

"No, sweetie, I'm fine. Is Jade here yet?" she asks.

"No, is she coming home this weekend? I just talked to her."

"How did she sound?"

"I mean I didn't actually talk to her, I instant messaged her."

She shakes her head. "Good Lord, I don't know how you young people think you're communicating with people when you use those computers and cell phones. You have to do more than type in a few words. You need to talk to people, not type at them."

"One of these days I'm gonna get you to text message on your cell phone and to email on the computer."

She laughs. It is the first time I heard her laugh all day. "In your dreams, sweetie, and speaking of dreams, I need to carry myself to bed. I've got an early day tomorrow."

My grandmom and I talk about her friend again and then me at the dance studio. After that we head up to bed. It was a long day with a lot of nothing going on. Hopefully tomorrow will be better.

CHAPTER 5

Is It Me Or What?

"There's no place like home. I used to think Dorothy from The Wizard of Oz *had the right idea. Click my heels three times and everything would be perfect. Right? Wrong! This isn't Kansas and this definitely isn't my home."*

—*Tumblr.com*

It's early Saturday morning and I head out first thing. It rained late last night, so the air smells really good, all fresh and clean. The clouds are still heavy, like it's about to rain again. I could skip it and stay in today, but I've been waiting for this all week. It's relaxing, it's invigorating and it's freedom.

Terrence turned me on to it and now I love it. It's like a drug, but you don't pay for it and you don't get high or anything. You get exhausted and you think. My music plays, but the sound of my breathing and my heartbeat is really what keeps me going. My feet pound the hard pavement, and I don't see anybody or anything. There's no destination, only the run in progress. So, I keep running.

So many things go through my head as I run. My hopes, my dreams, my regrets, they all come to me. I hope and dream all the time, but it's the regrets that always stay with me. I have a lot of them, and they go way back, back to my mom and her handful of pills, back to my sister who was my cousin all my life, back to my sometimes boyfriend Terrence, lawn mower guy, who I messed over big time. I know I can't change the past. I can only do what I can right now to make the future better.

I text messaged lawn mower guy three times last night. He didn't return any of my messages. I know I'm thinking about him way too much, and that's getting on my nerves. I've never let a guy get to me before. I wasn't even this attached to LaVon, my ex. I don't know why I'm trippin' about it now. He's just a guy, no big deal. I can do without him.

It starts to drizzle, so I turn the corner and keep running, heading back to my grandmother's house. My song comes on. I start smiling. It's a Tyrece jam and it's kinda like the music we danced to last night. The beat is pulsating and perfect for dancing and running. I turn the last corner heading back, and I see Li'l T across the street. He waves and says something. I can't hear him. I drop one of my earbuds to listen to what he's saying. "Hey, Kenisha, what's up, what you doing out this early?"

I nod and wave. He's with his boys already. "I'm running," I say, stating the obvious.

"From who?" he jokes.

Not funny. "What are you doing up? You just getting in from hanging out all night?" I ask him.

He smiles, loving it, like he really was out all night. "You know that's right," he says. His boys are dutifully impressed. "You going to VA today?"

"Yeah, later."

"Tell my girls I said call me."

There's no way I can answer that with a straight face. So I just wave and keep running. I smile, thinking about a few weeks ago when I punched him in the eye. Of course, it was an accident. I didn't know it was him. I was so mad. I was punching anyone around me. He just happened to be in the way. I get back to my grandmother's house and head up the front steps.

My body is weak and drained. My legs feel like rubber, but it's a good feeling and I'm energized. It's really starting to rain now. I hurry up the steps to the porch. Then as soon as I walk in the front door I head to the kitchen for some water. My grandmother's there. She's sitting at the table going through her bills. "Good morning, Grandmom."

"Good morning," she says, as she quickly glances over her shoulder. "How was your run this morning?"

"It was good. It started drizzling, so I cut it short." I grab a glass and get some water, then plop down in the chair across from her. I watch as she begins gathering her bills together. There are a lot, more than I expected to see. I notice there are several from a Health Institute. "What's all this?" I ask.

"They're bills."

"No, these—Northern Virginia Health Institute—what are they?"

"Now didn't you just answer your own question? They're hospital bills."

"I know that, but why do you have them? Have you been in this hospital?"

"I guess I've been in and out of just about every hospital in the area."

I know she didn't answer my question. Sometimes she does that and sometimes I just drop it, but not today, not now. I want to know what's up. "I mean are you sick?" I ask. The suddenness of having asked the question caught me off guard. Now I don't know if I'm ready to hear the answer.

"I guess I'm about as sick as the next person, I suppose."

"That's still not an answer, Grandmom," I say seriously. It's obvious she is avoiding the question. "Are you sick?"

"Don't worry about me, sweetie. Now, what time are you headed to your father's house today?" she asks, as she continues putting the bills away into a large envelope.

"Um, later this morning," I say.

"All right, I'm heading out in about an hour. I can drop you off if you want. Why don't you go up and get ready?"

I nod, then get up and leave. I'm no fool. I know she still didn't answer my question. I turn around and look back at her. She stands up and goes to the kitchen window. She's looking out. I'm not sure what kind of expression she has, but I get the feeling something's up. I go upstairs, take a quick shower and then change. Fifty-five minutes later, I head back downstairs and look around. If we're going out, my grandmother is always on time and ready. But she's not.

I go back in the kitchen and see her still standing at the window looking out. "Grandmom, are you okay?"

"Yes, I'm fine, just thinking." She turns and half smiles. "Are you ready to go?"

I nod, seeing she's been crying. My heart won't let me ask her again.

It rains the rest of the day. I'm not talking about that little bit of stuff that comes down in a mist. No, I'm talking about that heavy rain where you can barely get the windshield wipers to go fast enough. We went to my dad's office first and then we drove to Virginia. Since nobody was there, she dropped me at my dad's house, and I hurry to the front door and ring the bell.

It still drives me crazy that I have to ring the bell at my own house. I wait a few seconds. No one answers. I can hear the television inside blasting. I ring the bell a couple more times. There's still no answer. Next, I try the door knob. It turns. As soon as I open the door, I realize it's not the television blasting. It's Courtney.

She's upstairs screaming her head off as usual. I go in and listen at the bottom of the stairs for a minute to hear who she's yelling at. I should have guessed. It's my dad. And I can just imagine what the argument is about—money, other women and me. It's her standard trifecta when it comes to their fights, although not necessarily in that order.

Simply put, Courtney wants my dad's money. My dad gives her just enough to take care of the house, no more. She hates that. She knows my mom got whatever she wanted.

Then there are the other women. Courtney wants my dad
to be faithful. That's really not gonna happen. And then
there's the third one, me. She hates me. That's okay, 'cause
I hate her ass, too. I don't know what my dad expected to
happen when he introduced us. Me to like her? She's in
my house trying to take over—did he really expect best
friends? It wasn't gonna happen. Then, after I slapped her,
it was really on.

All of a sudden the argument gets really loud. I know
postpartum is supposed to be a bitch, but seriously, who
could tell the difference with Courtney's crazy-ass. She's a
raging, screaming lunatic most of the time. Apparently today
is no different. Either way, I don't feel like being bothered,
so I go to the family room beside the kitchen and see if the
boys are around. They usually hide there when my dad and
Courtney argue. I told them to turn the TV up really loud,
so they're usually parked in front of the television with a
DVD. Today they're not.

I head back to the front of the house, then cut through
the living room to go to my father's home office. I once
found the boys hiding under my dad's desk. I think that's
when we started getting close. I remember looking under
the desk and seeing their big brown eyes staring back at me.
They were petrified. It reminded me of myself. I hated it
when my parents argued. After that, the boys and I became
close. I was their big sister and their hero. I liked that. Also,
the office is where I usually hang out when I come here.
It kind of reminds me of my old house before everything
changed.

The rest of the house was cluttered with a mass of cheap

bargain basement furniture. I guess Courtney thought if she had more stuff scattered around, you wouldn't notice how cheap it all looked. She was wrong. The place looked a hot mess. All but my dad's office—that was nice. It looks almost the same as it did when I lived here with my mom. I open the office door and walk in and then stop instantly. There's this guy with music earbuds on sitting at my dad's desk.

I stand there and watch him for a minute or two, more 'cause I'm just shocked to see him there than anything else. He's tall and light-skinned and looks a little like my dad. The first thing I think is, damn, I have another brother. But then I know that isn't right. He looks too old. He has to be like about twenty. So, he's just sitting there going through my dad's computer like he owns the place. He hasn't noticed me yet. His eyes are glued to the screen. Whatever he's doing on the computer, he's really into it.

Then he looks up and sees me. His eyes widen in surprise. I know I startled him. Still, he has this annoyed expression on his face, like I'm interrupting him or something. He pulls out one earbud and presses a key on the keyboard. I look at him, waiting for him to say something. He doesn't, so I do. "Who the hell are you and what are you doing?" I ask indignantly.

"Who the hell are you?" he asks right back, with the same indignation. He pulls the other earbud out, cusses under his breath and then stands up.

CHAPTER 6

Anybody's Guess

"I'm so tired of getting it wrong. It seems every turn I take is the wrong one. Every move I make leads me to a dead end."

—*MySpace.com*

shit. He's way taller and bigger than I first thought. He gives me this threatening look, but for real, I don't back down. I smacked Darien, so I am seriously up to smacking him down, too. "I live here," I say, then drop my bag in the chair and then pull my cell phone from my jeans pocket, ready to call the police. "Who are you?" I ask again.

"You must be his kid," he says, looking me up and down.

"Excuse me?" I say, looking at him the same way.

"James's kid," he clarifies.

"And you are?" I ask again.

"Cash, I'm Courtney's brother."

I look at him suspiciously. *Figures*. Then yeah, I can kinda see it now. He does look a little like Courtney. They have the same eyes and mouth and definitely the same angry expression. It must be a family trait, to look perpetually pissed off. "My father's name is Kenneth," I correct.

"My sister calls him James," he says.

"Your sister's wrong. James is my dad's middle name."

"Yeah, whatever," he says dismissively.

"So what are you doing in here?" I ask, glancing at the back of my dad's computer monitor. That's all I can see from this vantage point.

"Getting away from them. What does it look like?" he says, then sits back down, more relaxed like he was when I first came in.

I nod. It makes sense. Anybody with half a brain would want to get away from my dad and Courtney when they argue. It's like listening to a banshee and a barking dog. He rumbles low and loud and she squeals in this high-pitched whine that comes out like ear-splitting screams. Together they sound like some demented rap duet. I swear they drive anyone within listening distance insane. All you want to do is get away from them. "Where are the boys?" I ask Cash.

"Out back." He motions out the side door that leads to the big backyard behind the house. "I figured they didn't need to hear all that, so I sent them out. I told them to stay close."

I nod again. At least it sounds like he has some sense. I used to hate hearing my mom and dad arguing, too. I'd turn the TV up or the stereo up really loud, so I didn't have to hear. I walk over to the sliding glass door on the other side of the office to see if the boys are okay. They're right outside the door playing with a toy basketball and hoop. They aren't really playing, just tossing the ball back and forth. They look so sad.

I glance up at the reflection in the glass door. I can see the rest of the office behind me. I look at Cash. He's watching me. He doesn't see that I see him. Then I look at the desk, then the computer screen. I assumed Cash was download-ing music, but he wasn't. There is one of my dad's company spreadsheets on the screen. It looks to me like he's going through my dad's company files. I turn back to the room.

"So, are you here this weekend?" he asks, pressing a key quickly to clear the screen, acting like nothing happened.

I don't think he exactly saw me looking at the screen's reflection, so I just play along. "Yeah, although maybe not," I say. I hear my dad and Courtney coming down the stairs, bringing the argument with them. They're really going at it, and it sounds like they're in the foyer or living room now. My dad's voice is getting lower which means he's ready to end this. On the other hand, Courtney's shrieks are shriller and sounding more and more desperate.

"…you ain't going nowhere until you make this right…"

"…who do you think you're talking to? You don't order me to do anything in my house…"

I smile. The idea that Courtney was still trying to con-trol my dad was comical. Apparently she hadn't gotten it through her head that it just wasn't gonna happen. My dad is stubborn and strong-willed. He's not the type of man to be pinned down or backed into a corner. Just because she keeps having his kids doesn't mean she owns him. If this is the basic argument, I know it won't last much longer. 'Cause chances are he'll walk out.

"...then what am I supposed to do..."

"...does it look like I care..."

Then their voices get even clearer. They must be closer to the office door. It's hard not to overhear everything at this point. My dad's obviously ready to walk out on the whole thing. I go back over to the chair by the door and pick up my bag. If he's leaving, I'm going, too. We need to talk.

"...and you need to tell your whores not to call my house..."

"...your house? Since when is this your house..."

Okay, now this argument I know all too well. It's the same one my mom used to have with my dad. It's all about control again. And my dad is not one to be controlled, particularly when it comes to him screwing around.

Cash and I look at each other. He shakes his head slowly. "You know he treats her wrong, don't you?" he says, obviously taking his sister's side in the argument.

I don't say anything at first. It seems strange to discuss it with him. I don't even know him. But I do know Courtney, and whatever my dad is doing, she deserves it. So I, of course, choose my side, too. "Well, maybe if she'd stop screaming like a psychotic banshee, he'd treat her better. But seriously, what does she really expect from him, to be faithful to her? She was doing the same thing to my mom that somebody else is doing to her right now."

He gives me this fierce look, so I had to add a little something, something extra. "What goes 'round, comes around. Karma's a bitch, ain't it?" That was for my mom.

Cash doesn't say anything. He just keeps looking at me. His eyes narrow. It's like he doesn't expect me to take my father's side or something. Idiot.

"...what am I supposed to do for money..."

"...get off your lazy ass and go get a damn job..."

After that, the argument burst through the office doors. Cash and I both turn, seeing them. Neither looks surprised or embarrassed that we'd heard them arguing. They do put the fight on pause for a minute. Courtney glares at me like she always does. I glare at her, too. Ever since I smacked her, she knows to stay out of my face. She said I was too much like my mom. Yeah, that's for damn sure.

Technically, she's just a few years older than me, but she always looks beat down, even when she's so-called dressed up. No wonder my dad was stepping out again. 'Course it doesn't explain why he stepped out on my mom with her in the first place. My mom was always looking good. But that's another story.

"There she is. If you don't have it, then make her get up off that money. You know she got it. Her mother left her all those damn insurance policies. Get the money from her."

I am just about to say something when my dad turns to Courtney. Their eyes lock. "You need to shut up," he hisses.

Out of all the times I heard my dad and mom argue and now Courtney and my dad argue, I never actually saw it before. When he turned to her and told her to shut up, I thought he was gonna beat her down. He looked that furious. But my dad's not a hitter. He will, however, walk out.

Courtney ignores his warning, big mistake. She just keeps on. "She needs to sign some of those policies over to us."

"You don't know what the hell you're talking about," I say, butting in. But the thing is, *I* didn't know what the hell she was talking about. Nobody had ever said anything to me about insurance policies or having money. I never even thought about it.

"Sign a policy over to *us?*" my dad repeats slowly.

"Yeah, to *us,*" Courtney yells back. "I'm part of this, too. Me and my kids deserve something. We've been together for over five years and I haven't gotten a damn thing out of it. You told me you had big money. So where is it? I know she got money and you keep giving her more. But me and my kids don't have anything. We walk around here in the same clothes all the time, eating spaghetti and tuna fish, while she gets whatever she wants. I'm sick of it."

I try not to laugh at this point. Spaghetti and tuna fish is all she knows how to cook. And she can't even do them right. But I think she expected to have a cook and a maid and a nanny or something like that when she moved in here. Reality check—she got nothing and apparently was still getting it.

"Fine then, you can leave whenever you want," my dad says to her. "And as for money, if you'd stop spending it on stupid stuff, you'd have something. Nobody spends money like you. You ain't rich."

"I hate you," she screams.

"Yeah, whatever," he adds, brushing her off. He walks over to me. He looks tired, but I can tell he's still happy to see me. "Hey, there she is," he says pleasantly, as if the whole argument thing never happened. We hug like we always do.

"Hi, Dad, how you doing?" I say.

"I'm okay. What are you up to?"

"Nothing much. What's she talking about, insurance policies?" I ask quietly, and then spare a glance at Courtney, who's eyeing me like she could kick my ass. Please, as if.

"Don't worry about it. It's nothing important. Everything okay with you, baby?" he asks, and then hugs me again.

I am just about to ask him about Hazelhurst when Courtney butts in.

"What do you mean it's nothing important?" Courtney yells. "Why don't you tell her what you told me?" I look at my dad. He shakes his head. "Your father thinks it would be best if we break up."

"That's not what I said, Courtney," he tells her. He turns back to me again like nothing was going on. "You gonna be around later, 'cause I gotta get out of here and take care of some things at the office."

"Oh, hell no, you ain't going out of here until we get this straight. Your skank-ass whores are just gonna have to wait."

Nobody says anything for a few seconds. I think everybody is just shocked. Courtney has a way of sucking the air out of a room when she opens her mouth like that. I just decide to talk to my dad and get the hell out of there. "Dad, before you go, did you pay the tuition for me to go back to Hazelhurst?"

"Ain't this a bitch," Courtney says rhetorically. "This

heifer got the nerve to come up in here looking for a hand-out."

"Watch your mouth, Courtney," my dad warns over his shoulder.

She ignores him. "No, Kenisha," she says bitterly, looking directly at me. "He didn't pay your damn tuition to go to some damn Hazelhurst. What he needs to be doing is taking care of his real responsibilities here, in this house. But he's not doing that, either." She looks at him ferociously.

I ignore her. "Did you pay it, Dad?" I ask.

"Now, tell her why you didn't pay her school tuition."

I look at my dad again waiting for him to say something. "We'll talk when I get back later this evening," he says. But I know my dad. This is his way of avoiding the issue. He's not coming back tonight. "I gotta go." He kisses my forehead and turns to leave.

"Dad..." I begin, but get cut off.

"James, are you gonna get up off some money or do I have to sue your ass for palimony and child support?"

He stops, turns and glares at her. "You can try, but we both know you don't want to do that, don't we?"

She opens her mouth, but then closes it instantly. Her eyes narrow in hatred. Okay, I don't know what's going on right now, but something definitely is. See, this is why I hate coming here. It's always Jerry Springer up in here. I know this is my home and all, but putting up with Courtney and all this drama gets on my last nerve.

"You know what, James..." she begins.

"Courtney, why don't you just chill," Cash interrupts,

speaking up for the first time since they walked in. We all turn to look at him.

"Stay out of this, Cash. It's none of your business."

"Courtney, just drop it," he says.

By now, my dad is walking out of the office. I follow him, brushing by Courtney as she's talking to her brother. "No, I'm not dropping anything. He needs to take care of his responsibilities."

"Dad," I say, still following. He stops and turns to me.

"Baby girl, I gotta get out of here."

"Yeah, I know. I get that, but what about me? What's going on with my tuition? I need to know."

"I'll take care of it next week."

"Next week is too late. The new semester starts Monday morning. Are you gonna pay it or what? I need to know," I say.

He looks at me. I can see the struggle in his eyes. "Kenisha…" Just then Courtney walks up. Cash follows. She starts yelling about money all over again.

"Tell her where your damn money is," she insists.

I look at her, shake my head and just start laughing. Seriously, she doesn't have a clue. All she can think about is money. For some reason, she got it in her head that when me and my mom left the house, or rather got kicked out of the house, we took all of my dad's money. What a joke. My dad knew, but he never said anything. He just kept letting Courtney think he had money. My mom told me the truth. I'm not saying that he didn't have it at one time. I guess he did, but that was a long time ago.

As for who's got money now, that's complicated. Jade told

me that our mom put money into a money market account years ago. Then the stock market tanked. I don't know exactly what's in it 'cause it's for me and Jade and I can't touch it until I'm eighteen years old and enrolled in college. The alternative is when I'm twenty-two. Either way, nobody's getting their hands on anything for a while.

"I'll tell her," Courtney says vindictively. "He's broke."

The baby starts crying. We all look at the monitor receiver on the living room coffee table. Cash walks over to Courtney. "Come on, let's get the baby."

"You go, I'm staying my ass right here," she says.

"No," he says adamantly. "Come on, Courtney, get the baby."

She glares at me one last time, then walks away with her brother. I shake my head. She is such a trip. I have no idea what my dad saw in her. But whatever it was, he sure as hell isn't seeing it now. I look at my dad. I can see it in his eyes. What Courtney said is true. At least some part of it is. "Why didn't you just tell me?" I ask him.

"I was trying to work it out," he says. "I know how much you want to go back to the school. And I know your mother would want you there."

"What happened?" I ask.

"The stock market messed me up pretty bad. Work is slow and things are just all messed up at this point."

"So what happens now?"

"You have to stay at Penn."

"No, not about me, about you, what happens with you?"

"I guess I'm gonna sell the house."

I sit down slowly. This is all of a sudden too damn real. Selling the house, my house, this wasn't supposed to happen. I know it's not really my home anymore, but it was once, and I still feel connected to it. This is where I grew up and where my mom and I hung out. Selling the house seems like letting go of everything I loved and everything I had left of her. I'm not ready to let go. "Isn't there something else you can do?"

"No, the business is going down fast. I can't compete with the big super chains. People just aren't coming in like they used to."

"Change the business," I say, "and make them come in."

He half laughs. "It's not that easy. I wish it was."

"What about the boys and the baby? They're your kids."

"I'll provide for them."

"And Courtney?"

"Her, too, although not as much as she wants or expects."

I nod. I know my dad will do right by his kids. He's always been a good father. He's a lousy husband and boyfriend I guess, but a good dad. I look over to the office door and think about Courtney's brother and what he was doing on the computer. "So, what's up with Cash?" I ask.

"Courtney's younger brother. He just served four years active duty in the Marines. He's on leave right now and crashing here for a few. He's supposed to do reserve duty for the next four years."

"So he's staying here," I say. Dad nods. Just then the

boys bang on the glass door in the office. I immediately go back into the office. They see me. They start jumping and screaming excitedly. Their little faces are smashed up against the glass. I can't help but laugh and smile. I open the door for them and they immediately grab my legs. "Hey, mashed potatoes, hey, creamed corn," I say.

"Kenisha. Kenisha. Kenisha." They start jumping, dancing and screaming all over again. Anybody would think that I never come around to see them. But I'm here just about every weekend. Although, now that things are changing again, I don't know how long that's gonna be.

"I gotta go," my dad says.

"Fine, we're going, too," I say, then turn to my little brothers. "Ya'll feel like eating pizza?"

CHAPTER 7

Making the Rules

"Just curious, who's in charge when there's nobody in charge? All this stuff going on and it seems like nobody's watching. What the hell is everybody thinking?"

—*MySpace.com*

MY dad takes me and my brothers to an early lunch. We eat at what used to be one of my favorite places. We're having a great time. We're like a mini family. The boys are crazy nuts and they eat like there's no tomorrow. 'Cause seriously, if I had to deal with Courtney's cooking, especially her spaghetti, I'd be starving, too.

But even though we are having fun laughing and talking, it's not like I've forgotten what he said about selling the house. And it isn't like he's forgotten his business is messed up. We just put all that aside and enjoy hanging out. We plan to talk about all that stuff the coming Friday. He's going to pick me up and we'll hang out. Later, he drops us off at the house and speeds out of there like the devil is on his tail. Maybe he's right, 'cause as soon as he turns the car around, Courtney comes raging outside. He was driving out of there and she was running after him. It would be comical, if it wasn't so damn sad.

She glares at me. I give her my own defiant stare. I know she isn't gonna say or do anything. She is a punk and she knows I know it. I hang out in my dad's office the rest of the afternoon. It's perfect. He has a refrigerator filled with junk and a full bathroom, so I'm cool. The boys hang with me. That always pisses Courtney off, so of course I encourage it. When it gets late, I go up to my bedroom to change for the mall. I open my bedroom door, turn the light on and go off. "What the hell?" I stomp down the hall to my dad's bedroom. The door is open and Courtney is sitting in the middle of the bed polishing her toenails. "What happened to my room?" I ask. She looks up at me and rolls her eyes, then goes back to what she was doing. "What happened to my room, Courtney?" I say again.

She doesn't look up this time. "I needed the space to clear away some junk in the extra bedroom, and since you weren't here, I moved everything into your room." She looks up at me and smiles. "You don't mind, do you?"

I am so pissed off inside, but all I do is smile and nod. "A'ight, fine, you got this one. But know this, whatever you think I got, I'll make sure you don't get a damn penny."

She looks up at me again. Her eyes narrow. I know exactly what she is thinking and all the names she is calling me. But I don't care. Letting her think she's messed up getting money is enough for right now. "You don't have anything I want," she says.

I smile. "Are you sure about that?"

"You wouldn't always be here begging, if you did," she says smugly.

I smile again, and this time I chuckle. "Are you sure about that? Why should I use my money when I can use my dad's?"

Her expression changes. This time it is obvious she isn't so sure. She gets pissed all over again. I love it. "You know what, Kenisha…" she begins, but I close the door and walk away. I can hear her screaming as I head back to my bedroom. She is getting louder and louder. I start laughing. I love messing with her. She always thinks she can get the best of me, but she can't. I go into my bedroom and look around. It is a mess.

To make room for her brother, Courtney, the perpetual bitch, screwed up my bedroom by dumping a whole bunch of her stupid junk in here. There are boxes everywhere. Courtney is a TV-ordering junkie. She lives for it. Every stupid thing she sees, she orders. My stuff is still there, but her junk is everywhere on top of it. Okay, I'll give her that point. But that's the last damn point she's gonna get. I change and leave after that.

I see my girls for a hot minute Saturday night. But I'm not in the mood to go to the movies or to even shop. We just hang out in the food court talking. They were really rooting for me to come back to school, so I need to tell them what happened. "My dad didn't pay Hazelhurst," I say.

"Is he going to?" Diamond asks. I shake my head no.

"Are you sure?" Jalisa asks. I nod, then look away.

"Shit." "Damm," they say, at almost the same time. I don't know who said what.

"Okay," Jalisa says, already thinking ahead. "What about a scholarship."

"Yeah," Diamond says excitedly, "yeah, a scholarship."

"Hell, no, I'm not doing that. You know that shit gets around. I don't want to hear it."

"Nobody's gonna know."

I look at her seriously. "We always knew," I say. Neither replied 'cause they know I'm right. We did always know and we pitied the girl on scholarship. She was like a poor relation coming to stay with a rich family. She never quite fit in, and we all kinda made sure of that. It was nothing we said, it was just there in the air. They knew it. After a while everybody knew and either shunned her or trashed her. I'm not really worried about being trashed. Ain't nobody at Hazelhurst that crazy, not even Chili or Regan. And being shunned isn't gonna happen as long as I have my girls with me. But I'm still not doing it.

The truth is I'm not about to hear all my old friends talking about me behind my back, 'cause my dad couldn't afford to pay the tuition outright. I'd rather stay at The Penn. A daunting chill slithers through my body. Staying at The Penn is hell, but I know I don't have much choice. Even if I apply for a Hazelhurst scholarship, it won't go through until my senior year. That means I'm at The Penn for now.

"Hey, how's Jade? Is she okay?" Diamond asks, changing the subject.

"She's fine," I say. Diamond and Jalisa look at each other. I know that look. They know something I don't. "What?"

"It was online and on Facebook. They broke up."

"What, please, like you believe what you read online."

"It was on TV, too," Jalisa adds. "Tyrece was with Taj. They were all hugged up talking about their plans. She was seriously pressed on him."

"Nah, they just work together. He's starting his production company and she just signed with him. It's all publicity," I say. Diamond and Jalisa nod, only half assured. I said it. I heard the words and tried to believe them, too. But somewhere in the back of my head, I don't. My grandmom asked about Jade earlier, and when I instant messaged her, she seemed distracted. But that was probably nothing, probably. "Jade and Ty are fine," I insist, maybe more for myself than for them.

"Kenisha." I turn around. It's Cash. He is standing behind me with two other guys. "Can we talk a minute?" he asks. The other two guys walk away. Diamond and Jalisa look at me. Jalisa's jaw drops. I nod and stand to walk to the side with him. "Look, I don't know you and you don't know me, but we're in the middle of the same mess with your father and my sister."

"No, we're not. Whatever's between them is between them."

"Nah, I'm not with that. It affects everyone in the house."

"I'm not in the house. I'm sure Courtney told you that."

"Okay, I get that you and Court have issues…"

"Issues," I repeat indignantly. "Is that what she said?"

"Yeah."

"Well, you need to tell her to clarify that for you."

He looks puzzled for a second, then recovers enough to

get back to his point. "What I'm saying is you two have problems. That's understandable. I know it must not be easy having your mom die and seeing your dad with somebody else."

I start laughing. "Don't be trying to psychoanalyze me. I don't have a problem. Your sister has the problem. She wants to control what she can't and she wants what she can't have. She needs to get over it and move on. Everything else is moot. As I said, it doesn't involve me. I'm not there enough."

"Squash that. You're there enough to know what I'm talking about. James needs to step up. Court has three kids, his kids."

"Again, all that's between them."

"So you're not gonna do anything?"

"About what? Talk to my dad about what—Courtney?"

"He needs to step up and put a ring on her finger."

I laugh again. This shit is so comical. "Why should he? Did my mom have one?"

"A'ight, a'ight, I get the fact that you're all pissed off about what went down between your mom and Court. But that's in the past. You need to step to your dad about that. Court had nothing to do with it."

"She put herself in the middle of their relationship. So what if someone else is doing the exact same thing to her? What goes around comes around." He can see the firm set of my determination. I'm not budging.

"It's like that, huh?" He looks at me, nodding.

I nod, too. "Yeah, it's like that." The whole conversation

is ridiculous. Why should I help Courtney? She hates my guts. And as soon as she finds out my dad is gonna sell the house, she's gonna be even more pissed. It is hard to not smile about that. She loves the house and couldn't wait to move her skinny ass in. It's almost worth losing it.

Cash walks away and meets up with the guys he was with before. I know Diamond and Jalisa are gonna be curious. They ask about him as soon as I walk back over and sit down. "His name is Cash. He's Courtney's brother."

"He's cute," she says, then pauses and looks at me. "Wait, you mean Courtney's brother, like in your dad's friend, Courtney?" Diamond asks. I nod.

"OMG, for real," Jalisa says. I nod again.

"What did he want?" Diamond asks.

"I don't even know. He was talking about me getting my dad to marry Courtney."

"What?" both Jalisa and Diamond say.

"Yeah, I know, like that's gonna happen in this lifetime. He's got to be crazy to even think that. Can you see me partying at their wedding reception?"

"OMG, we forgot to tell you about the party," Jalisa says.

Diamond opens her mouth and nods. "That's right. The party's next Friday."

I smile. I know exactly what party they are talking about. Every year since almost the beginning of elementary school, LaVon has thrown a party just after school starts. It's always private and by invitation only. Of course I've always attended, but this year somehow I doubt I'll be invited.

"Think I should crash it?"

We look at each other and laugh, then Diamond looks away and stops cold. "OMG," she says, her eyes widen and her jaw drops. She looks at us and shakes her head slowly. "It's show-and-tell time, kids."

"Show-and-tell time, excellent," I say. Jalisa smiles.

"Wait for it," Diamond says.

Okay, we do this all the time. One of us will see something or someone that's a must-see for the other two. Then we'll wait for the perfect time to do show-and-tell. Jalisa and I are sitting facing Diamond, and whatever she's seeing is behind us. I start smiling and Jalisa is ready to jump out of her skin. "Come on, what is it?" Jalisa asks impatiently.

"Wait, not yet. They're still walking in this direction."

"Come on, come on, hurry up," I mutter anxiously.

"Okay, quick, turn to your left," Diamond says.

We do. Jalisa's jaw drops just like Diamond's did. "Oh. My. God," she says.

I don't say anything. I am too stunned. It is LaVon, my ex-boyfriend. He is there with Chili, my ex-best friend. We watch them stop at a store window, then he says something to her and she laughs. He grabs her butt and leans down and kisses her. But he doesn't just kiss her. He must have had his tongue halfway down her throat, kissing her. I can't believe it. I turn back around. Diamond is looking at me. I look over at Jalisa. She is looking at me, too. "What?" I say.

"Kenisha, are you okay?" Diamond asks.

"Girls, please, yeah, of course I'm okay. It's not like I didn't know they were together. She's having his baby, right. So, she can have him. Believe me, they deserve each other."

"Yeah, we know that, but..."

"What?" I ask, 'cause they are both still staring at me.

"Are you sure you're okay?"

"What? Am I supposed to care about them? Well, I don't. So let it drop. Whatever, tell me about school, what's going on with Regan and her new hair weave?" Diamond and Jalisa start laughing. They reminisce about my fight with Regan and how I tore out her weave. I laugh, too.

We are still joking around when Chili stops at our table. She looks down at me and smiles. "Hey, what up, long time no see, Kenisha," Chili says.

We all look up at her. I seriously want to burst out laughing, but I don't. She is just standing there with her tummy in my face. LaVon and his stupid ass is looking around like he doesn't know anybody. He's such a jerk. But I don't care anyway, whatever.

Jalisa finally says something. "Hey, Chili, LaVon, ya'll out buying baby clothes?"

Chili looks at Jalisa, her eyes narrow. Diamond starts giggling. I seriously don't want to say anything, but I just have to. "Hey, LaVon, how've you been?" I ask as nice as I can. I smile like nothing is wrong. He looks at me and smiles back.

"I'm fine, how are you?" he says, obviously really shocked to see me acting so nice to him after all that stuff between us happened.

"I'm doing okay. School's good. You gotta stop by and see my new baby sister. She's so pretty."

"I bet. How's your dad?" he asks.

"He's fine. Business is slow, but he's doing okay," I add. Jalisa and Diamond watch us as we talk. I can see by their faces that they can't believe how nice I'm being to LaVon.

"My mom asks about you all the time," he adds.

"Do me a favor and tell her I said hi," I say sweetly.

He nods and smiles again. "A'ight, she'll like that."

After that, we start talking about his family and reminiscing about old times when we all went to school together. Diamond and Jalisa join in. We are all laughing and joking and having a good time, except for Chili.

Now the whole time we're having this nice polite conversation, Chili is standing there staring at us like she can't believe it. We're talking and completely ignoring her. Her eyes start to haze over and glare wildly.

"So you know I'm doing the party thing next week."

"Oh, really," I say, acting mildly surprised.

"It's Friday night at the house. You should come," he adds. Chili's jaw drops. It's like she can't believe what she's just heard. I can tell she is getting pissed off. That was the whole idea. It was always so easy to push her buttons. She hits LaVon's arm and he stumbles to the side and looks at her.

"Hey, what up with you?" he says.

"Hello, excuse me. Do you not see me standing here? What the hell you smiling and acting all nice to her for," she yells. "You with me now, remember that. This is your baby."

"That's debatable and you know it," he snaps back.

"I hate you," she rages.

"Hey, it was your idea to come over here. I'm just talking."

"That ain't talking. It's you trying to get with her right in front of me. I can't believe your stupid ass."

"Ah, girl, shut up and be quiet. Ain't nobody doing anything in front of you."

"Don't be telling me to shut up. I don't have to be quiet. You don't own me. I can say and do whatever I want."

"Damn, Chili, hormonal much?" Diamond mutters quietly, but everybody hears her. We all burst out laughing. LaVon laughs, too.

Chili really starts to freak out. She is furious. "I hate your ass," she yells real loud. Just about everybody in the immediate area turns around and looks at her.

"Just shut up," he says. "You're just mad because she got you. I told you to leave it alone, but no, you had to come over here and be starting something. You just should have left it alone," he says.

After that she really goes off on him. We can barely understand a word she is saying. 'Cause when she's pissed she talks really fast and it come out half English and half Spanish. LaVon just gives up on trying to calm her down. He walks away. She follows, still screaming and yelling at the top of her lungs. "I hate you."

We watch them leave. "Daaamn, girl, I cannot believe you just did that," Jalisa says to me, smiling like crazy.

"Did what?" I say, acting all innocent.

"Don't even act like you don't know," Diamond adds. "You smacked Chili down. I can't believe you did that. That was so cool."

They laugh. Okay, I laugh, too. I knew exactly what I was doing. My grandmother always says if you want to get back at someone, pray for them. Well, I'm not about to do all that. So, I decided to do the next best thing and just be nice. Who would have guessed it would work so well? We can still hear Chili yelling her head off.

"You know this is gonna be all over school tomorrow. She came over here to get in your face and start something and walked away looking like a fool. And LaVon…"

"I know. He went along with it. How'd you know he would?"

"Because LaVon is LaVon," I say simply. But for real, he probably still doesn't have a clue what he did that made Chili so mad. "He's clueless." We look at each other and crack up laughing. After all this time it's still so easy to get to Chili. I don't know why she even bothers trying to step to me. I always put her butt back down. Jalisa and Diamond start talking about Chili and her crazy-ass in school. I just listen as I start thinking about Chili and LaVon. I was okay with it, really. I knew all about them, but I guess it's one thing to know about them and another to actually see them together.

Truth is, I am kinda hurt. Not that I want LaVon back. I don't. It just reminds me of being with my lawn mower guy. I miss him. I miss us and I still don't know what I did wrong.

After that, I'm not much in the mood to talk anymore. They understand. So Diamond and Jalisa drop me off at my dad's house. I don't mention anything about my dad selling it. I guess I'm still hoping it won't happen. I sleep in my dad's office. He doesn't come home that night anyway. No surprise there.

Sunday comes and goes and so do I. I let go of the weekend fast. There wasn't much point in hanging on to it anyway.

CHAPTER 8

A Fast Start to Nowhere

"I look up and see that I'm right back where I started. No matter what I do or how far I think I've gone, I'm still back to the beginning. Two steps forward and five back, it's the starting line all over again."

—Facebook.com

I'm at The Penn on Monday morning. Who would have guessed? I guess I should have, but whatever. I keep a low profile and just drift through the day trying not to be here. I accept the fact that I'm not going to Hazelhurst, so I guess I might as well make the best of what I have here. I am in first period when a note arrives for me. Ms. Grayson wants to see me. Shit. I forgot all about her. I go to her classroom and see her sitting at her desk waiting. She looks up when I enter. I don't say anything. "Have a seat, Kenisha." I sit down. "I asked the counselor to sit in with us this morning. He should be here in a few minutes, but let's get started. How was your weekend?"

"Fine," I lie.

"Good. Any problems?" she asks.

"Look, Ms. Grayson, I know you have to do the whole 'Good Samaritan' teacher thing, but for real, I'm fine," I state, and then turn seeing this white guy walk in. He is tall and tanned with wavy blond hair and looks a lot like that guy from the movies. He says good morning and walks over, taking a seat on the other side of me. "Kenisha, this is Mr. Martin. He's one of the school counselors here. I spoke to him earlier and asked him to sit in with us. I hope that's okay."

I shrug. "Whatever. As I was about to say, I'm fine."

"It's okay to talk to someone, Kenisha," Mr. Martin says. "We're here to help you. We know adolescence is a difficult time. We just want to make things easier for you. You've gone through a lot in a short period of time, more than some adults have in a lifetime. As a school counselor, I'm here to…"

I tuned out as soon as he opened his mouth. Obviously no one is getting the point here. He keeps talking about how he can help me. Blah, blah, blah. Cut. Okay, I'm starting to get a little annoyed now. This is way too many people up in my business. I look down at my jeans and decide to ignore them. Mr. Martin keeps talking about being a teenager and how hard it is now compared to when he was growing up. News flash—who cares?

"Kenisha," Ms. Grayson interjects, breaking Martin's "this is my life" mini-drama-down-memory-lane tirade, "you're an excellent student. I checked your school records here and at Hazelhurst Academy." I look up suddenly and glare at her. What right does she have to go snooping through my records at Hazelhurst? She stops talking like she heard me thinking or something. She nods. "You're upset," she says. Martin looks at both of us like he missed something. Duh, he did. She knew when I looked up I was pissed.

"Yeah, why did you go through my Hazelhurst records? That has nothing to do with me being here."

"You know it does. As a matter of fact, it has everything to do with it. This isn't your school of choice, I understand that. But the fact remains, you're here. So as I see it, you have two choices. Deal with it and make the best choices you can or don't and fail."

We eye each other. I understand her completely. She wasn't talking about just failing her class or school. She was talking about failing at everything. Mr. Martin looks at her. He seems like he is in shock or something. "Actually, Kenisha, we have numerous programs we can offer that will allow you to..."

Ignoring him obviously isn't working. So, like a tiresome gnat, I need to swat his ass away from me. I turn to him. "Mr. Martin, I already have a psychotherapist. His name is Dr. Tubbs. He's in Virginia and I see him once a week. My counselor at Hazelhurst arranged it. So I really don't need another counselor trying to poke around in my head."

I see Ms. Grayson smiling out of the corner of my eye. She was trying not to laugh.

He smiles and nods. "Okay, then. I guess I should let you two ladies handle your business." He stands to leave having finally gotten my point. "But, Kenisha, know that my door is always open to you. If you need to see me, just leave class and I'll have a note sent to your teacher to excuse you." I nod. He glances at Ms. Grayson, then leaves. Now the way he looked at her made me wonder. Did they cook this good cop, bad cop thing up or what?

"Kenisha, have you ever heard of a congressional page?"

"No," I say.

"It's a very prestigious position and a very unique opportunity. Being a page can open all kinds of doors for your future. Every year a huge number of students apply to be pages or assistants on Capitol Hill. Only a few are selected. I'd like to submit your name for consideration, but I can't if you're going to persist with your attitude."

Okay, I have to admit, she got me curious with this page thing. "Don't you have to be related to somebody to do that?"

"No. As a matter of fact, relatives of seated members of Congress are specifically excluded from applying. You do, however, have to be sponsored by a member of Congress."

"And you know a member of Congress?"

She just smiles. Okay, I have no idea what that means. But all of a sudden I feel like I am being bribed. She doesn't answer my question, and after that Ms. Grayson keeps at me to talk and open up. I don't know what her drama is. It's obvious it's not gonna happen. Now I swear to God, I just feel like screaming. A few weeks ago everything was great. Terrence and I were hanging out, Jade and Tyrece were engaged, I was on my way back to Hazelhurst Academy and life was just about good. Now this. Now everything. The bell rings. I'm out of here.

The rest of the school day is more of the same. Students walking around mindless and teachers thinking they know everything. At the end of the day I see Troy in the hall. He mean mugs me. I just brush him off and keep walking. Thankfully, we don't have any classes together. As soon as the last bell rings I hurry to my locker and leave. I am probably the first person out of the building. I call my grandmother and tell her I am gonna stop at Freeman after school. The truth is, I really don't feel like being home right now.

I take a shortcut to Freeman and get there just as Ms. Jay is opening the doors for after-school classes. I walk in with her, and we talk a little bit as she goes to the office to give me a key to one of the private studios on the top floor.

"You're here early. Everything okay at school?"

"Yeah, everything's fine."

"Penn Hall, right?" she asks. I nod. "A junior?" I nod again. "And you're not going back to Hazelhurst this year."

"Nah, I'm gonna finish the year at The Penn."

"I'm glad to hear that. I went to Penn Hall high school years ago. Of course it's way different now than it was when I was there. How's your grandmother and Jade? I haven't seen either of them in a while."

"Everybody's fine."

"Good." She hands me the keys to the studio. "Lock up when you're done and drop the keys on my desk if I'm in class."

"Okay. Thanks, Ms. Jay."

I go up to one of the private studios on the top floor and dance awhile. But mostly I just look out the window and write in my recipe book. I would never have believed

I like writing so much. Dr. Tubbs said it's a good idea to write this stuff down. It's like a journal, but not really. I write thoughts, ideas, feelings and dreams all mixed up with recipes my grandmother gives me to try out. I just wrote about being back in The Penn. Now I'm just sitting and looking out.

I like being up high and looking down. I get a different perspective from my bedroom on the third floor at my grandmother's house and here on the fourth floor at the studio. It makes me feel like I'm above all the drama down there on the street below. But I also know the reality. I have to eventually climb back down and deal with all that crap.

An hour later, I still don't feel like going home, so I stop at the Pizza Place to get a soda and write some more. Ursula is just getting to work. She is early, so she sits and talks with me. "Hey, girl, I haven't seen you all weekend," she says, while sliding into the seat across from me. "How was it?"

"It was all right, I was just hanging out in Virginia. What about you?"

"I was busy like crazy. One of the girls here just quit. We're shorthanded again. So now I have more hours. You sure you don't want to get a job here? The money's not bad and the tips are usually nice."

"Why'd she quit?"

"Her mom made her. There was another break-in down the street over the weekend and she was scared this place might be next."

"What do you mean another break-in over the weekend?"

"Girl, didn't you hear? There's been all these break-ins in the neighborhood lately. It's been going on for the past two weeks. I heard it's like a crew of four or five guys doing it. Everybody's talking about it at school. The police think it's all drug related, but they say that about everything that happens in the hood. Can't it just be some stupid break-ins?" she asks rhetorically, getting all militant.

"Maybe it is drugs," I say.

"Nah, it doesn't sound like it to me. It's all too random and scattered, like a last-minute afterthought. It sounds like whosever's doing it are just playing games. They break in after hours but don't steal anything, not even money. They just drink soda and beer and eat stuff. But whatever, all I know is that they were talking to some of the guys at school."

"What, at school?"

She nods. "Yep, they think it might be guys from The Penn."

"Why do they think somebody there is part of this crew?" I ask, now more interested. Ursula shrugs. "Who did they talk to?"

"I don't know. That's just what I heard. I'm just glad D's still locked up or they'd be talking to his dumb-ass. I know they'd probably be looking at him, too. You know the cops came to our house when it first started, asking questions. It was like they were checking out all the usual suspects. I hate it when the cops come to my house."

That reminds me… "I heard he's getting out," I say.

She shrugs again. "I can't stand it. His dad is all pissed off that he's there. The night it happened, the cops came in our house and found drugs in his room. I wasn't surprised, although my mom was shocked. They were stuffed in his stupid trophies. When you broke one over his arm and dropped it, some of the little packages came out and they were just lying there on the floor. The police knew all about D. They were just waiting to pull him in. That fight with Terrence made it happen. You know he's still pissed."

"Drugs in the trophies, I didn't see any of that."

"Yeah, girl, the cops were threatening to seize the house."

"Oh, shit. Can they do that?"

"Oh, yeah, but they didn't do anything. Anyway, later I overheard my mom talking to my aunt about D. She said the assistant D.A. was talking about making a deal. But I don't know if he's gonna do it."

"What kind of deal?" I ask. The first thing I thought was he'd try to pin all this on Terrence, but I was sure he wasn't that insane.

"He could get less time if he talked. Apparently the cops want whoever he's working for. It's some guy in Montgomery County. I don't know him, but I used to hear D talking on his cell with this guy named Dantee all the time. I think it's him."

Shit. I know that name. Darien took me to his town house before everything happened. Dantee gave me the creeps. Seriously, he actually made my skin crawl. The two hoochies with him were acting all pathetic like they were scared to death of him. But for real, he was scary. He reminded me of some kind of modern-day slave trader or something. He was looking at me like I was a piece of meat. I guess I was supposed to act like I wasn't hearing anything, but I heard what they were talking about. Ursula was right, he was Darien's boss.

"So, is he getting out or what?"

"I don't know. I hope not. If you ask me, he's right where he belongs. I know that sounds harsh. I know he's my half brother and family loyalty and all, but I really hate his guts."

"I know what you mean," I commiserate.

"So I heard you got pulled out of first period."

"Who told you that?"

"Li'l T," she says.

"How did he know?" I ask.

"Girl, you know how Li'l T be playing like that. He knows everybody's business. I swear the FBI and CIA need to hire him."

I nod. It's so true. "It was nothing. Ms. Grayson, my U.S. History teacher, wanted to talk to me. That's all. Apparently, she doesn't like my attitude in her class."

"I didn't know you had Grayson. I had her freshman year for World Geography. She's nice. I like her."

"She's okay, I guess. She's just all up in my business."

Ursula nods and smiles knowingly. "I know that's right. But she means well. She likes helping students. It's her thing. Whenever you have a problem, go to her, seriously. Her grandfather is some big shot senator or something. And for real, she talked me down from trying to poison Darien's butt most of my freshman year."

I laugh. Knowing how Ursula hates Darien, I can just see Grayson trying to calm her down. "I guess it worked."

"Barely," she says. "But seriously, why don't you get a job here? I think you'd like it."

I think about saying no again, but I figure, why not? I was already back in The Penn, so working in the neighborhood wouldn't be that bad. And if money was going to start being tight with my dad, I needed to get a job now. "I don't know, maybe. Where do I get an application?"

"I'll get one for you." Ursula quickly grabs an application and I fill it out right then. There isn't much to it since this would be my first real job. I list working in the office at my dad's company as work experience and use my grandmother as a reference. I give the application back to Ursula, and she takes it to the owner. I am leaving when Ursula calls me back. The owner wants to meet me.

I go back to a tiny little office next to the kitchen and talk to the owner. I've been coming here forever, and I swear I had no idea this guy was the owner. We always spoke 'cause me and my girls were in here after dance so much. I thought he was just some guy who hung around working and getting free food. He was always cool with us, and he knew I was okay. All this is to say that I got the job. I still can't believe it happened that fast. They give me a large pepperoni pizza and I hurry home to tell my grandmother, but she isn't there. I go to the kitchen and put the pizza on the table. I get a slice and sit down to eat. I see my grandmother's bill folder on the table again.

Curiously, I open it and pull out the bills I saw earlier from the hospital. There are four of them and they total some insane amount of money. It was crazy that my grandmother owed that much money. I wonder about her health care insurance. She is old, she has to have something. Then I start wondering if she has some kind of major health issue. My grandmom looks completely healthy. Maybe she was sick before and she just never said anything to me. I wouldn't even know if she was.

So I start reading the dates and the diagnosis to find out what is actually wrong with her. As much as I can figure, the dates are all wrong. Whatever was going on happened before my mom and I moved here. Then I see that the bills aren't addressed to my grandmother, but to my mom. This is weird. My mom wasn't in the hospital. But she must have been paying my grandmother's bills. Now that she's dead, I guess my grandmother has to pay them herself. But then the bills are all addressed to my mom.

Then I start thinking about it. There were a lot of things I didn't know before. I grab my cell and call the customer service number on the bill. It's a recording. I hang up. I wasn't sure what I was going to say if someone picked up anyway. I put the bills back in the folder and leave. I call Jade. She still isn't picking up. I call my dad, thinking he might know something. He doesn't pick up, either.

The thing is, I usually have no intention of dealing in other people's drama. But I guess I don't have a choice. My grandmother, Jade, my dad, even my girls, Jalisa and Diamond, were having it bad. I know I need to step up.

I go up to my room and sit down on the bed to start doing my homework, and then I hear the first two steps on the first floor creaking. They always do that. I can always tell when somebody's coming upstairs. I call out to my grandmother to let her know I'm home. When I hear the door slam closed I go downstairs to check. Nobody is there. It's strange. I am just about to go back upstairs when my grandmother walks in the front door. "Hi, Grandmom. Was that just you?" I ask.

"Hi, sweetie, here take this bag. Was that just me where?"

I grab the shopping bag and follow her into the kitchen. I sit it on the counter and look at her confused. "Didn't you just come in a few minutes ago?"

She walks over and starts pulling stuff out of the bag. "No. Why?"

"Nothing, I just thought I heard you come in a few minutes ago. The steps creaked like when someone's going upstairs."

"This old house has a lot of creaks. How was school?"

"Not too bad."

"Are you okay with staying there for a while?"

I nod. I wasn't really, but at this point there wasn't anything I could do to change the situation, so why stress out about it? "I stopped at Freeman afterward and then went to the Pizza Place and guess what? I got a job there."

"A job, what are you going to do with a job?"

"Work like everybody else," I say. "I'm usually sitting around doing nothing most of the time, so I thought I might as well get paid for it. I'm working at Giorgio's Pizza Place."

"That was fast."

"I know. It just kind of happened. He hired me right on the spot. I start tomorrow, although I work mostly on the weekends. Is that okay with you?"

"Sure, as long as you keep up with your studies and your chores around the house. What about going to see your father on the weekends?"

"It'll be fine. I'm going back to do my homework." The phone rings just as I leave the kitchen. It's one of my grandmother's friends. I hear her laughing and know she'll be on the phone for another two hours. I go back up to my bedroom and sit down to start my homework again. That's when I get sleepy. I am just about to lie down when my cell rings. I check the caller ID, then answer immediately. "Hey," I say, happy and excited for the first time all day.

"Hey," Terrence replies. There is a slight pause. "How are you doing?"

"Fine, how are you?"

"I'm all right. So you want to talk or what?" he asks.

"Yeah, I do. What's up with you?" I ask, trying not to sound like I'm accusing him of anything.

"I got a lot of stuff on my mind, that's all. Things I gotta figure out."

"Like what? Maybe I can help."

"Nah, I doubt it."

"Is it about school?" I ask.

"Yeah, it's school, too."

I know Terrence isn't going to out-and-out lie to me. I know his character better than that. He'll avoid the answer, but not lie. "I thought you were doing great in school. You're magna cum laude, right? Doesn't that mean you're doing great?"

"Yeah, it's not the grades. It's just other stuff."

"Like what?"

"Like stuff."

"Is it 'cause Gia's at Howard, too?" I ask. He doesn't answer for a few seconds. I guess maybe he doesn't know I know. Seriously, how could I not know? I just didn't know everything.

"It's not about Gia."

"Then is it about me?" I ask, hoping he says no real fast.

"Look, it's just stuff going on, that's all, and this has nothing to do with her."

Yeah, I've heard this disclaimer before, but choose to tune it down for a minute. "It seems like it does. I'm not jealous or anything, but every time I turn around I hear her name. So, what's the deal with you two?"

"There's no deal. We used to be tight and hang out," he says simply.

He doesn't have to elaborate. I know what that means. They were boyfriend and girlfriend. "And now?" I ask softly, 'cause I still don't know exactly why he called me all of a sudden. Now I'm thinking it's to make this ending official. Damn.

"Now nothing. We go to the same school, that's all."

I'm no fool. I know he didn't answer my question. There is no way I'm letting it go like that. "When did you break up?"

"Right before you moved here to your grandmother's house," he says.

Suddenly I feel like fresh meat. I know about Terrence's past when it comes to Darien and his little brother. I also know he wasn't exactly the good guy next door. He had his issues. But I never thought about who he was seeing before I moved here. Now it's obvious. It was Gia. "Okay," is all I can think to say. Then the other question comes out before I think to stop while I'm ahead. "Did you two actually break up?" Shit, I can't believe I just asked that, 'cause for real, I'm not sure I want to hear the answer.

"It was understood," he says. Okay, a dozen more questions pop into my head. But he stops me before I can get the first one out. "I gotta go. I don't want to be late for work."

"What do you mean work? I didn't know you had a job. Where do you work?"

"Here on campus. I gotta go, I'll talk to you later," he says. And just like that he's gone.

So then I am just sitting there holding my cell phone in my hand and wondering what just happened? My mouth is wide open and I am just shaking my head. I slowly run the conversation over again in my head. What the hell does, *it was understood,* mean? What was understood? Maybe it wasn't understood. Shit. Was I just 'understood'? Did I just get played?

CHAPTER 9

Next Line Please

"I changed. I'm different. But now I see that nothing is ever really what it appears on the surface. That sucks. I always expect to see one thing and then something else comes up."

—*MySpace.com*

It *was understood.* The words haunted me all night long. By the next morning I was through. I knew I needed to drop all this drama and the best way was to run. I usually run in the mornings on weekends and then after school during the week. But I start my new job today, so I decide to get up extra early and run before school starts. I get dressed, put on my sneaks, hurry downstairs and step outside. I look around the neighborhood, then up at the sky. It doesn't look like the sun is going to make an appearance today. It is still mostly dark, but I can see the heavy clouds still hanging above the city. It's early and the weather is chilly and dismal. I zip up my jacket and walk farther down the front steps, looking both ways as I go.

The street is empty, but then it always is early in the morning. I know because sometimes when I can't sleep, I get up early and come sit out on the front porch. I like the peace and quiet. But right now I walk farther down the front path. From this vantage I can easily see at least eight blocks in both directions. The houses, mostly row with few exceptions, one being my grandmother's, seem to stretch out endlessly. As I start running and turn onto the main street, I can see that the streets are more crowded than I thought. There are people going to work, cars and busses everywhere, so I feel safe enough, even though it's still just before dawn.

For real, this is the best part of my day. My mind frees up and I start thinking about all kinds of stuff going on, but mostly stuff that's happening right now.

I run past the local library where my grandmother used to work and then volunteer. It burned down three months ago. They said some crazy homeless fool thought it would be a good idea to cook dinner there. I don't know what some people are thinking when they do stupid stuff like that. What did he think—he was gonna get his grub on and nobody would notice an open fire in the back of the kids' section? The really dumb part is that he died trying to put it out with his jacket, which was covered with alcohol. So he basically lit up like a torch.

All that makes me think about the hospital bills on the kitchen table. None of that makes any sense. Why would my grandmother's bill go to my house in Virginia? After our conversation, I knew my grandmother wasn't gonna tell me anything, so I decide to ask Jade. If anybody knows what's going on, she will.

It is starting to get late and I know I still have a full day of classes ahead of me, so I cross the street and turn back to the house. Then, while I am running in place waiting on the traffic light to change, I look down a side street and see this guy. He looks just like Brian, Jalisa's brother. I slow down, then stop running to see if I can get a better look at him.

A black car turns the corner and he turns around. I see it is him. I am just about to call out to him when all of a sudden he starts running. But not like me. He is running like the devil is on his tail. Down the street he turns another corner. The car speeds up and follows. Right then I know he is running from them. I run down the same side street trying to see what is up, but by the time I get to the same corner, both Brian and the black car are gone. I stop running and look around. Damn.

So I head back to my grandmother's house. Now I am thinking about Brian and Jalisa. She never talks about him anymore, but I know she thinks about him. As soon as I walk in the door I smell food. I go in the kitchen and my grandmother is cooking and Ms. Charlotte is sitting there with her. "Good morning," I say. Both of them look up at me. Ms. Charlotte has red eyes. She'd been crying. She mutters good morning, and then half smiles as she looks down at the teacup in front of her.

"Good morning," my grandmother says, smiling. "What are you doing dressed like that?"

"I went running this morning."

"This early in the morning?" she asks, surprised.

"I had some things I needed to work out in my head and running helps me. There was a lot of people out this early so I was okay," I say. She nods, then I look at Ms. Charlotte. She's still looking at her teacup. "Ms. Charlotte, I just wanted to say I'm sorry about your brother. I didn't know him well, except to wave and say hi. But he seemed like a really nice man."

She nods and smiles. "He was. Thank you so much."

"Okay, I'm a go get dressed for school. Remember I have to work tonight, Grandmom, so I'll be in late."

I go upstairs wondering what Ms. Charlotte is doing here so early. My grandmother's usually up and in the kitchen, but I've never seen her with company this early before. Anyway, I get dressed, say bye and walk to school. On the way I see Cassie. We look at each other. She is with two other girls, and she glances over at me. I don't say anything and neither does she. We're definitely not friends anymore. Unfortunately, this is the odd day so that means she'll be in my last period class.

My early classes are okay. I get through them without much drama. But now I'm basically sleepwalking through the rest of them because I'm so tired. I guess running before school wasn't such a great idea, 'cause all I want to do by sixth period is fall asleep and that's not a good idea in U.S. History.

So I'm yawning and in a daze trying to stay awake as Ms. Grayson hands the quizzes back from last week. Surprise, surprise, I aced it. "Is this class boring you, Ms. Lewis?" she asks when she puts my quiz on the desk. "Nah, I'm just tired," I say, then expect her to go into one of her rants about being prepared for class also means being mentally prepared. But she doesn't. She just nods and continues passing the quizzes out.

When she finishes, she starts talking about something and how some dead guy did something else to some other dead guy and we should all be happy 'cause the dead guys changed everything for us. Blah, blah, blah. Really, could this day get any longer?

So about a century and a half later, the bell rings. Finally, it's the end of the day. Everybody jumps like it's the start of a race. I leave class quickly hoping to get out as soon as possible. Apparently Cassie had the same idea 'cause she is right in front of me. I hurry to my locker, but I see Troy already there at his. He's by himself for once. I walk up. He doesn't say anything at first and neither do I. We stand there side by side doing our locker thing. Then he starts. "You think you're really smart, don't you?"

I know he said something and that he was talking to me 'cause he stopped what he was doing and turned in my direction. There was a lot of noise in the halls, so I didn't really hear what he said the first time. "What?" I say.

"You think you're really smart, don't you, or do you really think I'm that stupid?" he asks.

Okay, how am I supposed to answer that? "I never said you were stupid," I immediately correct.

"True," he says, then leans in closer so I can hear exactly what he is saying. "You just assumed it because I play football, right? Well guess what, Kenisha? My grade point average is four-point-two. My IQ was a hundred thirty-five when I was in the ninth grade. I knew exactly what you said the other day. I used to read medical journals like comic books when I was ten. So trust when I say, the teenage part of my brain is very well-connected to my hearing."

Shit.

"The only reason I didn't go to that lame private school with your boy LaVon is because their football team is a joke. And it would be just too damn easy to shine. At least here I have a challenge or two. Yeah, that's right, I know your boy. We had the same classes in elementary and middle school, but right now I choose to be here," he says. I guess I looked shocked. "You don't remember me, do you?"

"No, should I?"

"Yeah, you should. We went to the same schools in Virginia. Then my cousin was in some of your classes at Hazelhurst. You know my cousin."

I seriously don't know who he's talking about.

"Yeah, that's right. The one you fought that got your ass here. So the next time you want to get up in my face, I suggest you bring your boy with you, 'cause I don't mind kicking a girl's ass."

Shit.

He slams his locker door and turns to leave, and for some strange reason I decide now is a good time to speak up. "Big deal," I say.

He turns back and glares at me. I know if he hits me just once I'll be in a coma for the next seven years. "Yeah, that's right. I said, big deal," I hear myself repeating.

"You got a serious beat down wish, don't you?"

"You're smart, really smart. Fine, I get it. So, why don't

you act like it? You walk around here pretending like some cookie cutter jock from a stupid TV show. Why?"

"I have my reasons."

"Nah, not good enough," I tell him. "I bet nobody here even knows about your grades, do they? Not even your boys." I know I'm right just by looking at his smug expression. "See, why would you even do that?"

"Like I said, I have my reasons. Don't tell me, the pubescent fragments of your minuscule cerebral has disconnected from your auditory receptors?" he asks, repeating exactly what I said to him before.

I laugh. "Okay, very funny," I say. "Yeah, I heard you. It just makes no sense, and if you ask me, that's not all that smart."

He looks me up and down and shakes his head as he chuckles. "You know you trippin'. I just told you I would kick your ass and you gonna jump up at me. Are you crazy?"

"Oh, please, it was an empty threat and you know it. See, I know your little secret now and if you're as smart as you think you are, then it's more fun for you to have me around to watch you play your mind games on everybody else," I say. He starts laughing really hard now. It was just like I thought. His ego is way bigger than his so-called intelligence.

"A'ight, bet," he says, walking away.

I stand there shaking my head. This place is such a trip. I gather the rest of my stuff and get ready to close my locker. That's when I see Sierra and Cassie walk over. They stop at Troy's locker. Cassie glares at me like she has something to say. Seriously, I don't need this drama right now, so I just keep pulling my books out. "You just can't keep your hands off shit that don't belong to you, can you?" Sierra says.

I turn around. Sierra is standing there with her fists balled on her hips, eyeing me. Cassie is at her back smiling. I really hate that bitch. "What are you talking about?" I ask.

"I'm talking about you and Troy," she says, as if I should have already understood what she meant.

"I was just talking to him, that's all." Seriously, I'm not about to be fighting some girl over some guy, especially a guy that I could care less about.

"Talking to him about what?" she asks indignantly.

Okay, here's the part where I usually just get pissed off and go off on her, but I knew this wasn't about Sierra and me. It's about Cassie standing there with her. I know she set this shit up. It has her dumbass wannabe drama written all over it. "We were talking about his cousin, Regan. We got into it at Hazelhurst a few weeks ago."

"You did that?" she asks, half smiling, apparently appreciating my work.

"Yeah, I did that," I say.

"That was you who yanked her weave out?"

"Yeah, so, Sierra, if you're thinking I'm talkin' to Troy, then you and I don't have an issue. I don't want him, never did and never will and he sure as hell doesn't want me."

"That's not what I heard," Cassie mutters close to Sierra's ear as she turns, acting like she didn't say anything.

"Then you heard wrong, Cassie. And if you think you want to step to me, I'm here. Don't be trying to get Sierra to do your fighting for you. I will seriously kick your ass and you damn well know why. And I don't need no friggin' trophy to do it. Now you think you bad, you want a piece of me, come on." I shove everything back in my locker and slam the door, waiting for her to step up.

There is a moment of silence as other students start gathering around waiting. I swear high school teens can smell a fight about to go down from two miles away. Now all of a sudden there's a mini crowd standing around us. Sierra looks at Cassie, who is still looking at me. "I thought you said she was trying to play me," Sierra says.

Cassie glares at me. I can see the hatred in her eyes. Then she turns to Sierra. "She's lying just like she did with D. She lied on him and got him arrested." Everybody around us starts looking at me.

"I didn't have to lie on him and he got himself arrested."

"Bullshit, you told on him. Nobody else could have except you," she snips.

"Well, it wasn't me, so you can just keep on believing whatever you want," I say to her, then glance at Sierra. She doesn't say anything because we both know the truth. She told the police about Darien, not me. She rolls her eyes and walks away. Cassie is still standing there. "You got something else to say to me?" I ask Cassie. She rolls her eyes and walks away. Everybody else starts walking, too. So after all that, I grab my stuff again and go to work.

I get to Giorgio's Pizza Place early. Not surprisingly, it's already getting crowded since it's the local hangout for just about everybody in the neighborhood. And after school it's crazy. The place won a few awards as the best pizza in D.C. and had a couple of write-ups in the *Washington Post* and the *Washingtonian Magazine*. And even though it looks big, it is still really kinda small. It has booths along the edges and tables and chairs in the middle. There is a counter that spans the whole back wall with a few stools on each side. There is no formal dining thing with a waitress and stuff. It is all order at the counter and then find a seat where you can.

Troy and his football crew are there and so are Li'l T and his mini crew. Giorgio waves me behind the counter as soon as he sees me. He actually looks relieved I am there. He sends me to the back kitchen to grab a white apron and a cap. Ursula comes in right after me and another girl, Nita, after her. We quickly get our stuff together and go out front to start.

Giorgio gives me a quick overview, but I already kinda know the general idea about how stuff works from coming here all the time. But now it's all behind the scenes stuff I have to learn. So he shows me how to slice pizza and work the warming oven. I also make fries, fill drinks, get rolls ready for sandwiches and transfer the pizza pies to the front counters to cut them in slices. The major ovens and grills are in the back kitchen where they actually make the pizza. The dough and sauce is already made and in the refrigerator.

Since I don't know the cash register yet, I am working on the front line with Nita. That means I am getting whatever the customers ordered ready while Sierra and Ursula take the orders. They have me running around like crazy. It's so busy I barely have time to look up, but when I do, I see

Gia standing in line talking to some girls I recognize from the neighborhood.

Seriously, she is the last person I want to see, but it's too late. She turns around and sees me a second after I see her. She smiles and nods. I half smile and nod back. Then one of her girls leans over and says something in her ear. She responds and the other two turn and look at me. Obviously they don't do the "show and tell" thing me and my girls do.

When it is their turn to order, her friends place the order while she walks over to where I am working on getting the drinks ready. "Hey, you're Keysha, right?"

I look up over the soda fountain. "No, it's Kenisha," I correct. I hate when people get my name wrong, especially on purpose like I figure she just did.

"Kenisha, that's right. I didn't know you worked here."

"I just started," I say, dumping more ice into the cup, then sticking it under the soda fountain nozzle and pushing.

"I heard you were Ms. King's granddaughter. So that makes you what, Jade's cousin, right?"

"No, Jade is my sister," I say, getting the next cup lined up and ready for ice and soda.

"Oh, I didn't know Jade had a sister."

"She does," I say simply, trying to look busy even though it's obvious the place has calmed down a lot. Mostly everybody was either sitting and eating or just hanging out talking.

"And I heard you were hanging with D for a while, right?"

She says it loud enough for both Sierra and Ursula to

overhear. They turn and look at us. I glance at Ursula. I can see she is checking Gia out. "You heard wrong. I was never hanging with Darien. He was trying to get with me, but that wasn't gonna happen."

"So you got him arrested," she says, rather than asks.

"No," I say, putting the cups on the front counter harder than I expected to. Some of the soda splashes from one of the cup lids and spills on the counter. I grab a rag and wipe it up. "I didn't get him arrested. He got himself arrested. That had nothing to do with me." This conversation is getting old.

"But getting T pulled into that stupid shit did, right? You know they really messed him up after that, don't you? He didn't deserve that."

I stop what I'm doing and look at her. "What?" I ask. "How did he get messed up? Who messed him up?"

"Oh, he didn't tell you, oops, sorry. 'Cause he was telling me all about it the other night when we were together on campus. So I guess when I heard you and he were supposed to be hanging out, that was wrong."

Okay, I might not know much at times, but I know when someone's trying to play me. By now her other girls are standing there with her watching us. But at this point I really don't care. "You know what? Actually, you heard that part right. Terrence and I are hanging out. We are together."

"If you say so," she says, snidely.

"No, that's what I know," I say definitively.

"Yeah, okay, whatever," she says, then smiles sweetly, like

she knows something I don't. Then she walks away with her girls. She doesn't look back even though her two girls do.

"Hey, what's up, you okay?" Ursula asks, standing next to me now. She grabs a small cup and pours herself an iced tea.

"Yeah, everything's fine," I say, but I know differently. Everything isn't fine. Gia wants Terrence back.

"It can get a little crazy around here, but you did good."

"That's okay. I'm surviving. I'm used to crazy."

"So what's up with you and Gia? You know I never liked her," Ursula says, watching Gia and her friends as they sit down in a booth by the front window. "She always thought she was better than everybody else."

"You know Gia?"

"Yeah, she used to stay with her grandmother in the summertime when her parents were working in D.C. Then her family moved away, I think to Atlanta or something like that. Then I heard they moved back to the area, outside of Baltimore I think. She used to talk to Terrence a while ago. Then she hung out with D for a while. Then after that, she started hanging with Terrence again. Darien was too pissed about that. I think what it was is that she liked D 'cause he had money from his dad and other places. But I think she liked T because he's just a nice guy."

"So she and Terrence were together."

She nods. "As far as I know, yeah, but then I heard she dumped him when she moved away. Then you came and it was that whole payback thing with them all over again. Darien knew you and T were talking. I think that's why he was trying to get to you. It was payback for T taking Gia from him."

"I was payback," I say softly.

"Uh-huh, ever since the stabbing when they were kids they've been fighting each other one way or another. They fought over you like they fought over Gia before. So, I wonder who she wants this time." Ursula looks over, seeing someone walking up to the counter. "I gotta go."

She goes back to the cash register and takes their order, then we all go back to work. After that it gets a little busy again, but nothing like it was before. I see Gia and her friends get up to leave. I watch her go. She never turns back to even glance in my direction. Before Ursula wondered who she wanted back. I know the answer to that question. It was obvious. So as far as I'm concerned, the line is drawn. There is no way she's getting lawn mower guy.

CHAPTER 10

Do You Hear Me?

"Sometimes I feel like I talk and nobody hears me. I know they're out there, they're just not listening. Hey, I do have something to say."

—*Twitter.com*

It's still early when I get home from work. As soon as I walk in I see my grandmother sitting in the living room. The room is half dark with just a low light on in the corner. She isn't reading or watching television, she's just sitting there with her teacup beside her on the table. For the first time in a long time, she looks really sad and really old. The last time she looked like this my mom had just died. At the time, I was so into myself I didn't even realize I wasn't the only one hurting. My grandmother had just lost a daughter. I walk in and stand just inside the doorway leaning against the wall. I don't know if she even heard me come in. "Hey, Grandmom," I say, trying not to startle her. "I'm home."

"Hi, sweetie," she says, turning to look at me.

"Are you okay?" I ask.

"Yes, just a little sad I guess. When you get as old as me you get sad sometimes." She sighs heavily as she looks at the back of her hands, then turns them over to see the other side. I'm not sure what she's looking at or what it means.

"Are you sure you're okay?"

She nods. "Laurence's funeral is tomorrow night at the church," she says slowly. She looks back up at me. It is obvious to see she's been crying.

"Umm, I was thinking maybe I'd go with you. Is that okay?"

She smiles. "Sure it is."

I see the shine of gladness in her eyes. She isn't exactly happy, but I can tell she feels a little better. Then we don't say anything for a little while. "Do you want some more tea or something?" I ask. She shakes her head no, then assures me again that she is okay. Then we do the whole "how was your first day at work" and "don't let it interfere with your schoolwork" thing. After that I tell her I have a lot of homework to do, but really I just don't want to be there anymore.

I go up to my room and collapse on my bed and just lie there with my eyes closed. I don't know how long I lay there. I am thinking about my grandmother. She looked so troubled. I grab my phone and call Terrence, but don't get an answer. Then, what Gia said popped into my head. *Terrence had gotten messed up.* I have no idea what that means or even who did it. I sit up, grab my cell again and text him. I wait a few minutes for a reply. Then, figuring I won't hear from him anyway, I toss the phone on the bed beside me and open my English Lit book.

Just as I start to read *The Great Gatsby,* I hear the sound of constant ticking coming from the hallway. I get up and go out into the hall to look around. That's when I see Jade's bedroom door is cracked. She's hardly ever here anymore, and sometimes I forget this is her home, too. I walk down the hall and peek in. She is sitting at her desk on her laptop. I knock, push the door wider and go in.

"Hey, I didn't know you were coming home today. What are you doing here?" I ask, plopping down on her bed and genuinely happy to see my big sister. Jade always has a way of changing my perspective when I have a problem and making it better. Even though we didn't always get along as cousins, I think we're a lot closer as sisters. She looks up at me and then goes back to typing.

"Not now," she says vehemently.

"I was just asking a question."

"I'm doing nothing, okay, I'm minding my own business," she says sarcastically, without looking back up at me again.

I can tell this was going to be one of *those* conversations. We have them sometimes. "What's with the stick up your ass? Damn, I just came in to say hi."

"Yeah, whatever, hi," she says, in typical Jade style.

Okay, ordinarily I'd just walk away at this point. When Jade is in a mood, she can be brutal. And God help anyone in her way. But I know I haven't done anything to her, so I don't mind hanging around and prying. The alternative is reading the *Gatsby.* Anyway, I know something is up by the way she is so distracted and typing. "So like what, you can't mind your own business hanging out with Tyrece in

New York or Atlanta or L.A. anymore?" I say. She stops typing and looks up at me. I know right then what Jalisa and Diamond said was true. "Shit, it's true, isn't it? Ya'll broke up, didn't you?"

"Yeah, we did," she says, averting her attention back to the keyboard and monitor.

"Damn. Jade, I'm so sorry."

"Why are you sorry?" she half mutters.

"Just because I am, I guess. I thought ya'll were like the perfect couple. His eyes sparkled whenever he looked at you."

"Well, not anymore, I guess."

"So what happened?" I ask. She doesn't say anything. "Was it really Taj like they say?"

She stops typing again and turns around. I'm sitting on the bed watching her. She looks at me funny like she has no idea who I am. "Are you interviewing me now so you can blog or post this on some internet site?"

"What? No, of course not," I say, instantly affronted. I'm hurt she would even think I'd do that. "Why would you even say something like that? I would never tell anybody anything you told me, ever. We're sisters."

"Yeah, okay, fine, it's just that everybody I talk to about this winds up repeating it on Facebook or Twitter or someplace else. Everybody wants to know what happened between us. I'm so sick of all this stupid drama. We broke up. It's no big deal. People do it all the time. Right now, I just want to take the night off to hide from all of it. That's why I came here."

"Well, this is the perfect place to hide out. You know

nobody comes here except Grandmom's bingo friends, and you know what they're like. Reporters better not get in your face here." We laugh, knowing how intimidating and assertive our grandmother and her friends can be when they want to. "If you're hungry, I brought a pizza home with me. I'm working at Giorgio's Pizza Place."

"Yeah, I heard. Grandmom told me you were a working girl now. When did all that happen?"

"Monday after school, they had an opening, so I applied and got the job. It's no big deal really. I'm just getting pocket change to help out around here."

"You helping out, yeah, right," she says sarcastically.

"Yeah, I can help out, too," I say.

"So how are you going to work here and go to school in Virginia?" she asks, going back to her typing.

"I'm not. I'm gonna stay at Penn Hall."

"What?" she says as she stops typing. "Why would you do that? You finally got back into the school you wanted and now you're quitting and staying at Penn. What happened?"

"Yeah, I got in, but now Dad can't afford the tuition. Business is pretty bad with the economy slowing down and all."

"What about getting a scholarship or a school voucher?"

"Nah, I don't want that," I say.

"Ashamed or embarrassed?" she asks.

I nod. "Both," I say honestly. There isn't much point in lying to Jade or to myself anymore.

"I figured that, but I guess at least you owned up to it." She goes back to typing again.

"But it's not like I'm embarrassed and ashamed about getting it. It's how they're gonna treat me when I do, like they pity me," I say.

"You mean the same way you treated other scholarship students when you were there? You pitied them, didn't you?"

"Yeah, all right, I get it," I say. "What goes around, comes around, right. I always felt sorry for the scholarship students, so now all this comes back to bite me in the butt."

"All right, as long as you already know it," she says, smugly.

When Jade is in her shitty mood she is vicious and anyone around her is liable to get trashed in the process. "Yeah, whatever," I say, getting tired of her acid attitude. I get up to walk out. Then I stop. "I have a question for you. Did Mom have insurance policies or money when she died?"

"What?" she asks, looking at me again.

"Insurance money. Courtney was talking about how Mom had all these insurance policies."

"Who's Courtney?" she asks.

"Dad's girlfriend, the boys' and Barbara's mother."

Jade smirks. "I still can't believe he got her to name his baby after Mom. She must be an idiot."

"She is, but that's another story. Did Mom leave policies?"

"Yes."

"So where are they, where's the money?"

"Tied up," she says. "Nobody can get to it."

"Except you, right?" I say. She looks at me funny, like she was going to say something then changed her mind. "So what if I needed some of it now, how do I get it?"

"You don't."

"Why not?" I ask, determined to get an answer from her.

"Because it's for college. Damn, you are so selfish and self-centered, Kenisha. Just suck it up. Believe it or not, you're not the only one with drama going on in their life right now."

"I never said I was." I defend myself quickly.

"You didn't have to. I see what you're trying to do. You're trying to get money to go to Hazelhurst, right? That's all you ever think about—going back to your so-called 'perfect life.'"

"I said I was staying at Penn," I rebut forcefully.

"Only until you can find a way to go back there. But you're gonna have to find another way 'cause you're not getting access to the accounts," she says.

"Forget this," I say. I am headed out, but then it hits me to ask Jade about the bills. But right now, no way. "I don't need your help. I can do this by myself."

"Fine, do it," she says.

"Fine, I will," I repeat, then storm out. I don't need her anyway. As soon as I get to my bedroom I hear my cell phone ring. I grab it and answer. No one says anything at first, and then a few seconds later a female voice says my name. "Kenisha."

"Who's this?" I ask.

"You need to give me my money back."

"Excuse me, what?"

"You heard me. I want my money."

"You have the wrong number."

"I know who I'm talking to. You are Kenisha Lewis and I know where you live. I suggest you get my money, now."

I press the end button and drop my cell like it's on fire. My hands are shaking. I look around my bedroom quickly. I get the eerie feeling I am being watched. I look down at my cell again. I pick it up and press the last incoming call button. It registers as "Private Caller." My heart thunders in my chest, and my stomach quivers and flops. *WTF.* "What the hell was that? What money?"

CHAPTER II

What Lies Beneath

"Like ripples in a pond. Toss a stone and watch the result. Drama always goes big. Ultimately, there are more important things in life."

—*Twitter.com*

I never did do my homework last night. After that stupid phone call, I just laid back until I eventually fell asleep. I was fully dressed and the lights were still on when I woke up. So now it's lunchtime and I have exactly twenty minutes to read these chapters and answer the questions. I decide to hit the school library so I can concentrate. It's basically where all the nerd and computer geeks hang out reading comic books and talking computer stuff. Which translates to mean they're hiding and trying to avoid getting beat down. I figured it didn't matter since they'd be in their world and I'd be in mine.

So I am sitting in one of the back areas of the library trying to avoid drama, and don't you know drama comes right over and sits down right next to me. Well, not actually next to me, but close enough. Drama is standing two aisles over and right behind where I'm sitting.

At first I'm not paying any attention to what they are saying. I figure it is either some horny couple wanting to do their thing in semiprivate or a couple of idiots reading out loud. Then they kinda get louder, 'cause now they are almost arguing. It sounds like it is two guys and a girl and it takes me a few minutes to figure out what they are talking about. They are bragging about how they broke in someplace and how they are planning on doing it again this weekend. My jaw drops. My mouth is wide open. I can't believe what I am hearing. The first thing I think about is when Ursula told me the police were questioning students about the break-ins in the neighborhood. *Oh, shit.* I seriously should not be here right now, if they see me...

Then, even though my cell was on vibrate, it still makes a noise. Somebody is calling me. I grab it and stuff it in my pocket. Apparently they didn't hear it because they just keep right on talking. I don't really recognize any of the voices. But I know if I stay they'd know I was there and heard them talking. There is only one way out of the back area and one way in. I quickly gather my stuff and ease around the table. Just then, a couple of other students come running through the aisle laughing and throwing something between them.

The conversation ends abruptly and one of the guys comes out from behind the stacks. Peeking through the books, I see who it is, but at the time he doesn't see me. The two kids playing around run past me and bump right into him. A slight shoving match begins as threats of bodily injuries are leveled. "What the hell are you doing back here, punk?" Boyce demands. Neither one of the two guys responds. They look like ninth graders and I swear they are about to pee their pants. They are petrified. But hell, I would be, too. It was Boyce. "I asked you a question, bitch," he adds.

One kid starts crying, and the other mumbles something I can't hear. They are both scared to death. "Damn right, nothing. Now get your asses out of here before I kick 'em," he demands.

Boyce is focused on threatening the two kids, so I turn around and pretend like I am just getting there. I try to ignore what was going on by quickly sticking my earbuds in my ears. I sit down and open my *Great Gatsby* book, ignoring everybody. But for real I am scared, too. See, this is why I hate this place.

Everybody eventually leaves. They ignored me, thank God. So I stay there the rest of the period. My earbuds are locked in, but my music is off. I still don't do my homework. I am looking around at the shelves of books and wondering what the hell I am doing here. This isn't my school and this isn't my world.

My cell rings again. I look at the caller ID, but don't answer since most people usually have sense enough not to call me during school hours. It reads, "Private Caller." My heart jumps. Yeah, there is definitely no way I am answering. I turn my phone all the way off and stick it in the bottom of my bag. A few seconds later, the bell rings. I almost jump out of my skin. Two more classes and the day will be over. But hell, it is only Wednesday.

I leave the library and head to English Lit. I still didn't

do my homework. It's no big deal since our teacher doesn't even collect it and just tells us to use it as a study guide for an upcoming test. My last class is Chemistry. The teacher is crazy. He jokes the whole time we're there. We study the periodic table and periodic law. Believe it or not, I really like the class.

By the end of the day, I am through. I don't go to my locker since I'm really not up for dealing with Troy and his boys. I don't have to work, so I go home and just chill out online with my girls. We instant message each other for about forty minutes and then my cell phone rings. I look at the caller ID. I tell my girls I'll catch up with them later and then answer. "Hello."

"Hey, it's me," Terrence says.

"I know, hi," I say, a little shocked by the phone call.

"What's up?"

Seriously, how do I answer that question? But he doesn't wait for an answer. I'm not sure if that's a good thing or a bad thing. "I heard you got a job at Giorgio's," he says. Of course I knew Gia told him. Who else would?

"Yeah, yesterday was my first day."

"How was it?"

"It was a lot harder than I thought it would be," I say honestly. "There's a lot of running around and filling things up and whipping things off. I made about a million French fries." He starts laughing. The sound of his laughter reminds me of better times when we used to hang out together.

"Yeah, I remember that part," he says.

"What do you mean, you remember it? How?"

"I worked at Giorgio's a couple of years ago. He still calls me in if he gets really jammed up and I'm available."

"I didn't know you worked there before."

"There're a lot of things you don't know about me."

"Yeah, I guess I'm starting to see that," I say. "I saw Gia last night. She was there with some of her friends. She told me you were in some kind of trouble. So what's going on? Is this trouble what you never want to talk to me about?" I ask. The line goes silent for a while. "Are you still there?"

"Yeah, I'm here. Gia shouldn't have said anything to you."

"She didn't. She just said you got messed up. She didn't elaborate. Are you gonna tell me what's going on, what you told her?" I say, emphasizing the last word.

"It's no big deal. I'm taking care of it."

"So you're still not gonna tell me." Again the line goes quiet. I know he is still there this time. "Fine," I say.

"Look, don't worry about it, it's over."

"Okay," I say. He obviously isn't going to tell me, so I let it drop, again. "So, how'd you know I was working? Gia tell you we talked?"

"Nah, Li'l T told me."

I smile to myself. "Figures, he knows everything about everybody. I wanted to tell you myself, but I wasn't sure if we were…" I don't end the sentence.

"You weren't sure if we were what?" he prompts.

"If we were talking or if it even mattered. You and I aren't exactly hitting it off the last few weeks. Ever since that thing with Darien that night we've been kind of off."

"It's just things in my head I needed to get straight."

I don't say anything this time. "So are we gonna be okay, still friends?" I ask tentatively.

"Yeah, we're okay," he says impatiently. "But I gotta go."

"Are you gonna be around later?" I ask.

"Yeah, the funeral's tonight. I'll be there."

"Yeah, me, too, I'm going with my grandmother. She and Mr. Russell were really close."

"Are you going to be okay?" he asks.

"What do you mean?"

"Your mom's funeral was just a couple of months ago."

"Yeah, I know. But I'll be fine," I say. I know already that isn't true. I really don't want to go to this, but my grand-mother needs me and I'm not sure what kind of mood Jade will be in. So I need to be there for her.

"A'ight, I'll see you tonight."

"Okay, see you," I say, then hang up and feel a lot better.

The service is at six-thirty, so by five o'clock I start get-ting dressed. I put on black pants and a gray cardigan and matching top. When I go downstairs, I see Jade is there. We haven't really said anything to each other since our "talk" in her bedroom the night before. Truthfully, I don't know what to expect. I know she is going through her thing, so I don't want to bother her with my drama. "You look nice," she says, looking up from her BlackBerry.

"Thanks. You do, too," I say. Seriously she does. I know Tyrece used to buy her expensive stuff. She always hated it because she was afraid people would say she was using him for his money. So that's why she'd never dressed over the top. But tonight she looks like serious money. She has on designer everything and diamonds.

Thankfully, the conversation is kept short since our

grandmother comes into the room seconds after I do. She looks at both of us and just starts crying. I instantly well up, too. We know what each is thinking. The last time we all stood in the living room like this, we were going to my mom's funeral. She opens her arms and Jade and I fall in. I don't know how long we stay there like that, but it is awhile and it feels good.

"All right, ladies, we need to make a move," my grandmother says. Jade and I nod. "You both look so beautiful," she adds still tearful. She touches our faces gently and smiles. "Your mother is so proud of you, almost as proud as I am. She so wanted to tell you everything. So, don't be too angry at her. She always did the best she could. But you know love doesn't always turn out like you hope it would, no matter how hard you try or work at it. But know this family is always, always, always, here for you.

"Just look around this room. This is your family and these are your ancestors. For better or for worse we are one. They stood in this room just as you stand here now. And in decades to come your children, grandchildren and great-grandchildren will stand here, too, God willing. Cherish each other, you're sisters and you're family. That always means something. And now that's it for that recipe." She hugs us again. "Thank you for being with me tonight."

"Of course, Grandmom, there's no place else we would be," Jade says sincerely as I nod my complete agreement.

After that we go to the funeral and then to Ms. Charlotte's house to pay our respects. There seems like there are a few hundred people there, but all I can see is Gia holding on to Terrence. I hate funerals.

CHAPTER 12

Getting It Right Ain't Easy

"Hearts racing, pulse quickening, breath panting. I love roller coasters. I always have. The spiral twists and sharp turns spinning out of control were exhilarating. It was exciting and scary all at the same time. I just don't like it when the roller coaster is my life."

—MySpace.com

I got back to my life the next day, and the rest of the week went by fast. I went to class, worked and studied and did all the things I was supposed to do. Friday afternoon I came home from school and planned to just chill the rest of the weekend. I didn't have to go to work until Saturday, so tonight was just gonna be about me. I had already made plans with my dad to go to Virginia, so he was going to pick me up and we were going to talk. I just needed to find out what time he was picking me up.

As soon as I walk up the block I see that my grandmother is home. She's sitting on the front porch with Mrs. Harrison from next door and Ms. Charlotte from down the street.

They are talking, laughing and drinking iced tea. It is good to see my grandmother smiling and laughing again. She seems to be really sad lately.

I walk up and say hi to everybody and kiss my grandmother on the cheek. They all respond happily and ask about my day. After that they go into a whole conversation of what it was like when they were in school. Mrs. Harrison's story is the most fascinating since she grew up in Hawaii. Mrs. Harrison is our next-door neighbor and also Terrence's grandmother.

I knew he had another ethnicity in him, I just didn't know what it was, and he never really talked about it so I never knew. She told stories about growing up on the island and how she came to live here in D.C. It was pretty interesting. But after a while they started talking about how everything had changed and I really didn't want to hear that, so I tell my grandmother I'm gonna go pack and get ready to meet my dad.

Since I decided to go to LaVon's party, if only just to piss off Chili, I know I need something good to wear. I haven't been shopping in forever. But I already have a lot of clothes, so I'm cool. I pick out some skinny jeans and a retro Run-DMC T-shirt and then pack something to wear Saturday morning. When I'm done, I call my dad to see what time he's going to pick me up. He picks up on the second ring. "Hi, Dad," I begin. "How's it going?"

"Hey, baby girl, you okay?" he asks.

"Yeah, I'm fine. I was wondering what time you're gonna pick me up today. I figured we could hang out before I go to LaVon's party tonight."

"Ah, baby, we can't do it today. I meant to call you earlier to let you know I'm not in D.C. I've been in New York all week."

"New York," I say surprised. "What are you doing there?"

"I'm trying to put some things together for the business. I'm talking to some old friends about doing some work. It looks like it just might be working out. I'll be here the rest of the weekend, so we're gonna have to postpone hanging out today."

Big surprise, this is so lame. My dad has been blowing me off for as long as I can remember. I know I should be happy because he's being proactive about getting his business back together, but I was really looking forward to talking to him. "Okay, I understand," I say, trying not to sound as disappointed as I am. "Good luck with all that."

"But, hey, the boys are still looking forward to seeing you. They said something about going to a movie Saturday morning."

"Yeah, I know. But it's no big deal. We can do that later."

"Now you know they don't understand the concept of later. They're kids and it's a big deal to them," he says, then pauses a few seconds. "Baby, hold up, let me call you back in a few."

Surprise, surprise, this is so typical. "Nah, that's okay, Dad. I'll see you when you get back, or whenever," I say, before ending the call. I sit on my bed and push my overnight bag to the side. This isn't what I expected, but it's so my dad. Kenneth James Lewis is the ultimate old school player, so whether or not he is even in New York was debatable. He's always so single-focused on his life, and that's it. Nobody else really matters as far as he's concerned.

I grab my stuff and start hanging it up again. Then it hits me. Screw this. I'm going to Virginia anyway. I decide to take the Metro, then just get Diamond to pick me up. I can either stay at her house or Jalisa's. I start putting my clothes back in the bag when my cell rings. It's my dad. "Yeah," I say.

"I got you a ride to the house. Cash is in D.C. right now."

"What?"

"You met Cash, he's Courtney's brother."

"Yeah, I know who he is. I just didn't want him picking me up. Look, Dad, that's okay. We'll just get together and talk later and I'll see the boys then."

"No," he insists. "I don't want to disappoint the boys."

"What?" I say. Shit, he disappoints me, his daughter, all the damn time.

"Is there a problem?" he asks.

"Yeah, there's a problem. I don't want to be dealing with Courtney and her stupid drama this weekend. You're not gonna be there and I don't want to hear her mouth. And if she brings up my mother one more time, I'm gonna smack the shit out of her. She's your thing, not mine."

"Where the hell is all this coming from?" he asks.

Oh, please, is he kidding me? Like he doesn't know I hate her guts. But instead of saying that, I just stay quiet. I don't feel like having this conversation with him right now. Seriously, it can't be a total shock that his baby momma and I don't like each other. Hell, the second time I saw her I slapped her. Remembering the stunned look on her face after the slap still made me smile all over again.

"Look, baby girl, you won't be dealing with Courtney. She's with her mother this weekend. That's why Cash is in D.C. He just dropped her and the baby off."

"So the boys are with her there, right?" I surmise.

"No, Cash has the boys."

"Dad, do you even know who this guy is and you just let him take your kids like that? I don't get it. He could be some crazy pedophile or something."

"He's not. He's okay. I've known Cash a long time. He used to work at the office when Courtney worked there."

Okay, this story is getting more and more insane.

"Cash is really a nice guy. And since he got out of the Marines, he's grown up a lot. When he was younger, he used to babysit the boys all the time when Courtney and I wanted to be alone together."

Whoa, did he just say that? Does my father not have a clue who he's talking to? Hello, I'm his daughter, the one he used to ignore when all this was going on. He never had time for me and my mom, so now I know why. Cash was babysitting while he was screwing Courtney. Okay, this is just too much and I have to say something. "Oh, you mean the times when you were supposed to be home with me and Mom, right? When we were supposed to be hanging out like a family, right? When Mom and I would beg you all the time to take us out with you, right?" I say. I swear I just all of a sudden blow. I don't mean it to sound as angry as I am, but whatever. It is all the truth.

"Baby girl…"

I quickly interrupt him. "Dad, you know what? Never mind. Forget this. I don't want your apologies and I don't want to have this discussion with you. You did your thing and made your choice, fine, whatever."

"Baby girl, it wasn't like that, listen…"

I interrupt him again. "And I'm not your baby girl," I almost yell. "Not anymore. You have a new baby girl, remember?"

"Kenisha, you will always be my baby girl."

"Thanks." I don't say anything else. I just press the end button. He calls right back. I see the caller ID and ignore it. I am tired of the whole stupid conversation. I can't believe I thought things were getting better between us. Everything is still the same. Nothing changes. It just gets buried underneath and comes out even worse. My dad calls three more times. I don't answer any of them. I am through.

I stay in my room just messing around after that. I refuse to be depressed. I call Jalisa and Diamond and tell them plans have changed. They agree to pick me up at the Metro stop later. I repack my bag and head downstairs. As soon as I am halfway down, the doorbell rings. I hear my grandmother coming out of the kitchen to get it. "I got it, Grandmom," I say and open the door. As soon as I do Jr. and Jason, my crazy little brothers, run into me. "Hey, cookies and milk, what are you guys doing here?" I ask, calling the kids the made-up nicknames I always give them when I see them.

They hug me and of course start arguing over who is which. "I'm cookies," Jr. says.

"No, I'm cookies," Jason responds. "You're milk."

"No, you're milk, I'm cookies."

A second later they see my grandmother standing in the kitchen doorway behind me and their faces light up all over again. They half run, half walk down the hall to her. I turn to see her bend down as they get to her. They grab and hug her and both start talking at once asking for cookies and cake.

"Hey." I turn back around, seeing Cash standing there. He smiles. "May I come in?" he asks.

I don't know what I was thinking. I completely forgot somebody had to bring the boys to the house. "Oh, yeah, sure, come on in," I say.

He comes in and glances around. "Wow, your house is really nice. It's huge."

"It's my grandmother's house. You're living in my house."

"Look, I'm getting a little tired of this. Why can't we just call a truce? Neither one of us agrees with the situation or is willing to do anything about it. So let's drop it. All that other stuff is between James and Court."

"I didn't know you knew my dad before."

"Before when?" he asks.

"Before when my mom and I lived at the house, before your sister got my dad to kick us out, that before," I clarify.

He shakes his head. "So much for the truce," he mutters.

"Yeah, ya think," I say.

"Look, I just came by to give you a ride up to the house."

"You mean my house?"

"You want to let that go?"

"No, not really," I say.

"Good afternoon, and who do we have here?" my grand-mom says, as she walks down the hall to where we are still standing in the foyer.

"Sorry, Grandmom, this is Cash. Cash, this is my grand-mother, Mrs. King."

"Good afternoon, ma'am, my name is Cassius Lawson."

"As in Muhammad Ali, Cassius Clay?" she asks.

"Yes, ma'am, my grandfather is a huge boxing fan."

"He's Courtney's brother," I add.

She nods. "I see," she says, without any outward rec-ognition. "Well, nice to meet you, Cassius. The boys are in the kitchen having cookies and milk. Can I get you something?"

"No, ma'am, I'm fine, thank you."

"So why are you two standing here in the foyer? Come into the living room." She turns and walks into the living room, taking her favorite seat by the fireplace we never use. We follow.

"He's not staying, Grandmom," I say.

"I just came by to pick Kenisha up. James asked me to give her a ride to the house."

"I guess he didn't call you. My plans have changed. I don't need a ride anymore."

Cash looks at me. "Are you sure?"

"Yeah, I'm sure."

Jr. and Jason come into the living room smiling like sweet little cherubs. They each have a small brown paper bag in their hand. "We got cookies for tonight," Jr. says. Jason nods happily. "We gonna see a movie next."

"Actually, guys, I can't take you to the movie tomorrow. We'll have to do it another time," I say. The disappointment in their faces is obvious. I hate doing this and I know my dad was right, they don't understand "later."

"I'll tell you what, I'll take you to the movie tomorrow, okay," Cash says.

I guess he expects them to be just as excited going with him, but they aren't. Going to the movie with me wasn't just hanging out and seeing a movie. It was a whole day thing at the mall and then at the playground and then to get ice cream and sprinkles. I kind of feel bad seeing their faces now. "I'll tell you what, I'll stop by the house and we'll hang out later," I tell them. They brighten instantly.

"Good, now that's settled," my grandmother begins, "Cassius, would you like some cake or cookies for later?"

"Yes, ma'am, thank you."

"Kenisha, why don't you take Cassius into the kitchen and get him a slice of cake and some cookies?"

"Sure," I say begrudgingly, then turn and walk to the kitchen. Cash follows.

"That was kind of wrong, not taking them to the movie because you had a fight with your dad."

"You have no idea what you're talking about and none of this is any of your business anyway," I say, hacking off a hunk of cake for him. I wrap it in plastic wrap, then I stuff some cookies in a bag and give it to him.

"Thanks."

I don't say anything. We go back into the living room and

he thanks my grandmother again and says his goodbyes. I give the boys a hug and promise I'll see them soon. They hold their bags close and smile happily enough.

After they leave, my grandmother remarks about the boys as she always does. "They're such sweet little guys," she says. I nod. "I need to make sure I give your father's friend the cookie recipe, so she can bake cookies for them sometimes."

"I don't think that's gonna happen, Grandmom," I say. "Courtney isn't exactly the Betty Crocker type, if you know what I mean. She cooks spaghetti that comes out looking like zombie brains." I start laughing remembering my dad actually trying to get me to eat with them. To my surprise, my grandmother starts laughing, too.

"Well, no never mind about that. I started out the same way. We all do. My first meatloaf looked like a huge raw meatball. It took five hours to cook it. By the time it was fully done inside the outside looked like the bottom of an old shoe." She laughs again. "She'll get better in time."

"No, she won't," I say, as we laugh again.

"Okay now, so what are your so very important plans this weekend that you don't have time to take those boys to a movie?"

"I'm meeting my girlfriends Jalisa and Diamond tonight. We're going to a party. Then I'm spending the night at Jalisa's house. Her mom and grandmom will be there."

"You're not staying at your dad's?"

"No."

"Why not?" she asks casually.

"He's not going to be there this weekend. He says he's in New York trying to get his business together."

"That's good, isn't it?"

I shrug. "He started talking about how he and Courtney used to hang out on weekends years ago and Cash would babysit the boys for them."

"While you and your mother waited at home for him," she surmises.

I nod. "Yeah, he didn't even realize that those were the same weekends he'd tell Mom and me that he was away on business. But he was really with her all weekend. I couldn't believe he was telling me all that."

"So you don't think he's in New York now."

"That's just it, I don't really care. He's probably someplace starting a whole new family all over again."

"You can't change anyone else's behavior, Kenisha. You know that. You can only change yourself."

"I know. It just makes me so mad that he lied to us all those years ago. And Mom never did anything about it. She never called him on his lies."

"Oh, she called him on it, all right."

"Then why didn't she do anything?"

"Like change him?"

It hit me what she was getting at. It was exactly what she just told me. You can't change other people, only yourself. "Why didn't she leave him?"

"She didn't want to upset your world."

"You mean the world where we got kicked out of the house anyway and my mother died. That world," I say sarcastically. She frowns at me for my disrespect. "Sorry," I apologize.

"We all try to do the best we can with what we have. If we succeed, wonderful. If not, we just keep trying. Remember that."

"I know. It just makes me sad sometimes."

"I know, sweetie, it makes me sad sometimes, too." Neither of us says anything for a few minutes. Then my grandmother changes the subject. "So now you need a ride to Virginia, right?"

"No, I'm gonna take the Metro and Diamond will pick me up. I'm all packed."

"Do you want a ride to the Metro stop?"

"Okay," I say. I hurry upstairs and grab my cell phone and bag. By the time I get downstairs, my grandmother is ready to leave and so am I.

CHAPTER 13

The Frenemy of My Enemy is My Friend

"There are good ideas and there are bad ideas and then there are really, really bad ideas, but sometimes there are to-die-for brilliant ideas. This is that time."

—*MySpace.com*

LaVon Oliver lives two blocks from my dad's house. Jalisa lives around the corner and Diamond around the corner from her. So we are all pretty much in the same neighborhood. We've known each other since we were all kids together. We've fought together, played together, cried together, argued together, but most of all, we've laughed together. And that's what we do tonight. We laugh.

We get dressed at Jalisa's house since both Diamond and I are spending the night there later on. I wear my Run-DMC T-shirt and jeans with my Nike sneakers. I have my hair down and straight. Diamond and I spent all afternoon doing it. It looks great, but there's no way I'm keeping it like this. It's way too much trouble to do it.

"It looks great like that. You should just get a perm and straighten it for good," Jalisa says.

I look in the mirror and shake my head. My hair bounds long and straight down my back and over my shoulders. It looks nice, but definitely different. It doesn't even look like me anymore. "Nah, I'm not going through all that. I like it curly."

"You know, of course, Chili is going to freak the hell out when she sees you walk in there tonight," Diamond says.

We laugh, knowing it was the only reason we were going to the party in the first place. Although we'd drop by LaVon's house for his parties the last few years, we never stayed long. After a while, it always turned out to be the same thing. Some idiot would get into a fight with some other idiot and take it out in the street. It would get crazy loud and then the neighbors would call the police and all hell would break loose.

"Chili freaking out, I can't wait," I say happily.

"I just want to make sure I get her face on my cell phone so I can put it up on my Facebook page," Jalisa adds.

"Ooh, and I want a video, too. So, come on, we need to go. By the time we get there, everything will be over," Diamond says, putting on her lip gloss and then stuffing the tiny tube into her purse.

We hurry downstairs. Natalie, Jalisa's older sister, is in the family room off the kitchen with her two kids. They are watching *Monsters, Inc.* for the hundredth time. "Ya'll look really nice," she says. Her two kids never turn around.

"Thanks," we all three say.

"What time are you getting back?" Jalisa's mother asks.

"We're not going be out too long. A couple of hours at LaVon's parties are pretty much all anyone can take," Jalisa says.

"Are you going to take the car?" her mother asks.

"No, we're gonna walk. There's probably no place to park anywhere near the house. We're going now. See you later."

"Have fun," Natalie and Jalisa's mom says, just before we close the front door and scream, "Bye."

As soon as we get outside, we burst out laughing, then start walking down the driveway to the main street. On the way, we talk about school and hanging out like we used to. "I can't believe you're not going to be coming back to Hazelhurst," Diamond says.

"I know, right," Jalisa agrees, "we were all supposed to graduate together and then go to college together."

"Well that's still gonna happen. We're going to college together," I say.

"What about the money? College is way more expensive than Hazelhurst Academy. But I guess you can get some scholarships or get a student loan or something like that, right?"

"Nah, my mom left me money for college. Jade told me."

"For real?" Diamond says. I nod. "Good."

"Man, can you believe how old we're gonna be when we get out of college?"

"We're not gonna be that old."

"Old enough," I say.

"Okay, we'll get our undergraduate degree and then our graduate degrees. Then we'll get married."

"No, wait, you forgot the traveling part. We're supposed to travel first before getting married."

"That's right."

"Okay, undergraduate degree, graduate degree, travel and then get married."

"And then have kids," Diamond says.

"But we have to time it right if they're gonna all grow up together. Man, can you imagine us as parents, as moms?" We start laughing. The idea was so far-fetched. We had promised each other a long time ago that we'd chill and abstain from sex.

We reaffirmed our pact to not start motherhood until we were at least twenty-five. That meant we'd be out of college for a few years and we'd be traveling on vacations together for another few years before we settled down. Twenty-five was the perfect age.

"Deal," we all say, agreeing.

"Oh, my God, I forgot to tell ya'll, I got a job," I say.

"What!" both Jalisa and Diamond say. "Get out. Where?"

"You'll never guess. I'm working at Giorgio's Pizza Place."

"Are you serious?"

"For really?"

"Yeah, I started last Monday. I like it, but it's so hard. I thought it was going to be easy, but it's not."

"Do you make the pizzas?"

"Nah, Giorgio has real cooks that make them. I'm usually on cash register or on the line."

"What's the line?"

"That means I'm putting the orders together."

"Wow, I can't believe you're there."

"And guess what? Terrence used to work there, too."

"Really?"

I nod.

"How are ya'll doing?" Jalisa asks.

"The same. He's not talking and his old girlfriend, Gia, keeps hanging around. Ursula said Gia used to hang with Darien, too, back in the day. Now they both go to Howard and all of a sudden she's trying to get around him again."

"What, she trying to get him back?"

I shrug. "Truthfully, I really don't know. It looks like it to me. Her great uncle died and I went to the funeral with my grandmother. Afterward at the house, Gia was all over Terrence, acting all sad and holding on to him all night."

"You know she was just wrong."

"For real, is he tryin' to play you?" Jalisa asks.

"Nah, but I don't know. Gia told me that he got messed up, but she didn't elaborate and he's still not talking."

"That's so weird. So what did she mean by 'got messed up'?"

"I don't know."

"You know who might know," Jalisa says.

As soon as she says that, we all know the answer. Li'l T.

We turn the corner and see all the cars parked down the block. The houses are big with lots of land around them. You seldom see neighbors out 'cause everybody keeps to themselves. Music is pouring out of the house and lights are on in the backyard.

"Are ya'll ready for this?" Diamond asks, as we walk down the front path toward the house. We nod, laugh and walk inside.

Okay, as soon as we walk in, you can tell the party is crazy. It is already jumping. I swear you can hear the music two blocks away. There are kids in the living room, dining room and just about all over the house. But mostly everybody is outside in the back. It looks like everybody in Virginia showed up. We head to the kitchen and family room area and then out back on the deck and by the pool.

LaVon's house is huge and his backyard looks like a city park. Even though it is kinda cool out, the pool is open and a lot of people are in bathing suits playing around. We are saying hi to some of the kids we know as we walk through the house. Of course, we find out by the time we get there we've already missed two fights.

LaVon is there as soon as we step outside. "Hey," he yells and points at us from the other side of the deck. "You came."

Some kids turn around to see who he's talking to, but mostly everybody just keeps on having fun. We wave and he waves back. A few minutes later, he comes over to Diamond and Jalisa. I have my back to him. "So where's your girl?" he says. "What, she couldn't make it?"

Both Jalisa and Diamond look at me, puzzled. I turn around and I look at him like he's nuts. "Hey, LaVon," I say.

He looks down at me and I swear his eyes bulge out and his tongue hits the ground. He does a double take. "Damn, girl, look at you. What happened?"

"What do you mean what happened?" I ask.

He keeps staring at my face like he doesn't know me. "You look great, girl. What did you do to yourself? You look like a damn model or something."

I roll my eyes. This is so typical LaVon. "Yeah, thanks," I say.

"No, for real, you look really, really nice."

"Yeah, thanks," I repeat.

One of the girls Chili hangs with sees us talking and quickly walks away. We know what she's gonna do. Both Jalisa and Diamond pull out their cell phones.

"So what you been up to?" LaVon asks, still staring at my hair and face like he doesn't know me.

"School and work, that's about it."

"Oh, check, you working now?" he asks.

"Yeah, at Giorgio's in D.C.," I say.

"So you're really staying there for good now, huh?"

"Yeah, I am. It's my home and I like living in the city. Everything is right there for you and there are a million things to do." I did like the city, but definitely not the school.

"Yeah, like get murdered or carjacked," he says laughing. Several kids standing near us had started paying attention to our conversation and laughed along with him. Then a few other kids start doggin' D.C. and talking about how dirty and corrupt it is. I'm not saying they're all wrong. There are some pretty uncool places in D.C., just like every other city in the world. But D.C., for better or for worse, is my home, so I speak up.

"Well, I don't know about all that. I've never had any

problem there that I didn't have here, too. Yeah, they have drugs, but hell I've seen more drugs right here in the schools. It's not just the city and ya'll know it." They start laughing and agreeing with me.

"Anyway, I really like the city. I'm even gonna apply to be a congressional page next semester." I didn't exactly lie. Ms. Grayson did say she wanted to submit my name for consideration. And it did sound kinda interesting.

LaVon stares with his mouth open, and both Jalisa and Diamond look at me surprised. I didn't tell them I was thinking about it, 'cause I wasn't at first. Not until this exact minute. But when LaVon and the others were doggin' the city, I had to say something to impress them, and since Ms. Grayson did mention it, why not? "Oh, my God, for real?" Jalisa says.

"That is so cool," Diamond adds. "How old do you have to be to do that?"

"You have to be at least sixteen years old and get good grades."

"How do you get to do it?"

"Basically you have to know somebody and my grandmother knows tons of people. But my history teacher is the one who suggested it. I think she has some kind of pull on the Hill."

"Do you have to live in the city to apply?"

"No, but it looks good if you do." I lie this time 'cause I have no idea if you do or not. "I'm sure if you live in the DMV it's all right."

"The DMV," some idiot says, laughing hard. "The Department of Motor Vehicles, what the hell is that?"

I look at him, giving him my snootiest expression. I shake my head and sigh. "The DMV is an acronym for D.C., Maryland, Virginia. I thought everybody knew that."

The guy looks at me hard. I know he must be feeling like a fool. I smile. "I know you were just playing around," I say laughing. He laughs, too, knowing I just saved his butt from looking like a complete jackass.

So now everybody is looking at me like I know something. The fact is, everybody who lives in the DMV knows having an "in" in D.C. politics is primary when living in the D.C. area. It isn't what you know, or really how much money you have. In D.C. it is all about connection and who you know and how close they are to power. Suddenly, looking at their faces, I am the "it" girl, the closest one there to power.

We start talking again about politics and living in D.C. This time people are seriously giving D.C. the props it deserves. We are all laughing and joking, then out of the corner of my eye I see somebody I didn't expect to see walk over. He is smiling as he approaches. I guess he just got here, 'cause he is shaking people's hands as he walks through. When he gets to our group, he shakes LaVon's hand and they bump shoulders.

"Yo, it's Kenishiwa. I almost didn't recognize you, girl, looking all glam and shit," Troy says. "How come you don't do that at The Penn?"

"You just answered your question. It's The Penn," I say.

He nods, agreeing. "Yeah, you right, you right."

He has two of his boys with him, including Barron James. He introduces them, and LaVon introduces Diamond and Jalisa. Barron used to talk to Diamond for about a minute. But then she backed off for some reason. I notice Troy immediately locks on Jalisa. "So, what are you doing on this side of the Potomac?"

"Yo, my boy LaVon told me about his little soirée, so I thought I'd check it out for a minute."

Just then, a pushing scuffle breaks out inside, and we all turn around to see what's going on. "Damn, I hate these stupid ass fools. Always gotta break something up in somebody else's place. I'm not having this shit. Here, hold my soda," LaVon says, giving me his can. Then he hurries inside to break up the fight.

We all watch, trying to figure out what is happening. It looks like they were arguing over playing the video game, *Need For Speed*. We all start laughing as LaVon pushes them apart, and they are still arguing over who rammed the other into a barricade. They settle down when LaVon takes the *Need For Speed* game disc out and puts in *Super Mario Brothers*. He comes back over, laughing, and a few minutes later Chili shows up with two of her girls. She looks at Diamond and Jalisa. "What ya'll doing here?" she asks. I am guessing she doesn't recognize me 'cause she seemed to only be talking to Jalisa and Diamond and I had my back to her.

"Here's your soda, LaVon," I say, handing him the can. I turn around right after Jalisa and Diamond get ready.

"We're hanging out chillin' like everybody else," I say. "Hi, Chili. How you doing?" I toss my long straight hair over my shoulder like she always does.

"You remember my girl, Kenisha, don't you?" Jalisa says.

Chili finally sees I am standing there next to LaVon. Then just like LaVon, her jaw drops and she does a double take when she recognizes me. Her mouth never closes. I smile. Jalisa takes her picture while Diamond has already started her video of the whole thing on her cell phone. All in all, it's the perfect reaction. Then it gets even better.

"What the hell are you doing here?" she asks. Then she looks at LaVon and starts yelling. "What the hell is this bitch doing here? You said she wasn't coming. What the hell is she doing here?" She keeps asking him louder and louder and everybody around us starts turning around and laughing.

Now LaVon is starting to get pissed. Girlfriend or no girlfriend, he hates to be embarrassed. Chili is all up in his face, pointing her skinny fake-nail-wearing finger in his chest. She is screaming at him now, and she starts pushing at him. Even her girls are trying to get her to calm down. She is making such a commotion that LaVon's dad comes outside to see what is going on. He tells Chili she is going to have to leave.

She really gets pissed then, 'cause everybody is laughing at her. So now she is cussing LaVon and his dad out. "Oh, my God, no, she didn't just do that," I say quietly, still crackin' up.

"Oh, yes, she did," Jalisa mutters right next to my ear.

She is still going off and in LaVon's face when his mom

comes outside. The music instantly stops. Chili pushes LaVon, and he bumps back into his dad. "What the hell is this?" his mom says. Chili pushes LaVon again. This time he doesn't budge. "Oh, no, no, no, you need to get this little girl out of my house now, this minute," LaVon's mother says, then grabs Chili back, stepping in her face.

Chili shrugs away forcefully. "Get off me," she yells.

"Look, you. I don't care if you think this baby is my son's or not, you need to get up out of my house now. And I don't ever want to see your face around here again, understand? Out! Now!"

Chili calms down enough to realize it is LaVon's mother she is arguing with now. "But I didn't do nothing," she starts screaming and crying. "It was her, she started it." She points to me.

LaVon's mother looks at me. "Kenisha, is that you?"

"Hi, Mrs. Oliver," I say. "For real I didn't do anything. I just said hi to her when she walked over."

"That's the truth, Mrs. Oliver. All Kenisha said was 'hi' and 'how are you,' then Chili went off on LaVon and started pushing and hitting him," says Diamond.

"But it wasn't my fault. She's not supposed to be here."

"Is this your house, little girl?" his mom asks her.

"No," Chili answers tearfully.

"Then who are you to tell somebody they don't belong in my house?"

"But it wasn't like that."

"Do you want her here?" Mrs. Oliver asks LaVon while nodding at Chili.

"No," he says flatly.

"You son of a..."

Mrs. Oliver turns back to Chili. "Good night, little girl. It's time for you to leave my house now."

Chili turns and starts cussing her out in Spanish as she walks away. To her surprise, LaVon's mother answers her back in Spanish. Chili turns around. She is bright red. I guess she didn't know LaVon's mom is from Puerto Rico and she speaks Spanish fluently. And since a lot of his family is there, so do half the partygoers. They are telling her off in Spanish, too. She keeps looking around, getting more and more pissed. "I hate you, LaVon."

"Are you two with her?" Mrs. Oliver asks Chili's two girls, who were trying to hold her back when she was pushing LaVon.

"No, ma'am," they lie.

"We came separately, but she drove."

"She doesn't need to be driving home by herself."

"I'll go with her," her other friend says, as she glares at the two other so-called friends. "I'm still her friend."

The music comes back on, and the party resumes like nothing had ever happened.

After that, we didn't stay that long. I danced with Troy and LaVon. Jalisa danced with Troy and a few others and Diamond danced with Barron the whole time. There was another pushing fight, and we didn't want to press our luck anymore. We left and laughed all the way back to Jalisa's house. Jalisa copied and transferred her photos to my phone, and Diamond did the same with the video she took. We didn't know it at the time, but she caught everything. The three of us watched our video on our phones and laughed all night long. I love coming to Virginia.

The next day I pick up the boys, and we watch *Monsters, Inc.* at Jalisa's house with her sister's kids. We eat popcorn and pizza and have a blast. The boys love it and so do we. Then we do *The Lion King* and *The Princess and the Frog.* I get the boys back home late in the afternoon. I catch the Metro back to D.C. and have just enough time to shower, change and get to work.

CHAPTER 14

Ending on a Bad Note

"I was blindsided. I had no idea this night was gonna end like this. I'm still shaking. It's crazy. I keep seeing all of it playing out in my head. It rolls like a constant rerun. I still can't believe it all went down."

—*MySpace.com*

saturday night at work is crazy busy. There is a concert at the middle school around the corner and Freeman Dance Studio had a recital for their beginner classes. Added to that, there was a late-night sale at the shopping center across the street. All in all, there are about a million people coming in and out of the restaurant. I am on cash register duty most of the night, but I also do phone orders and work on the line. By the time I am about to take my break, I expect my feet to be numb, but I guess I am still pumped because of last night. I am energized and still feel great.

Last night was a trip. I didn't ever remember having so much fun at one of LaVon's parties. I watched the video from last night when I was on break eating my burger and fries. Ursula came in and saw me laughing, so I showed her the video, too. We laughed and I told her what had started everything.

"So wait, is it really your ex-boyfriend's baby?" she asks.

I shrug. "I have no idea, and truthfully, I don't really care. She can have him. They deserve each other."

We look at the video one more time and she makes me promise I'll take her to LaVon's next party. I agree. I go back to work after that. Sierra goes on break and I take her place on register. Just as I finish my first order, Gia steps up. I smile happily like nothing is up, but really I want to kick her ass just because. We say hi and do the whole nice girl thing. But I know she was hating on me the same way I was hating on her.

Ursula is working the line, so she is getting Gia's order together while I am taking the next order. But still I hear Gia ask Ursula about Darien. I could tell Ursula didn't want to hear it, 'cause she kept working with her back to Gia. "I heard he was getting out soon," Gia says.

Ursula shrugs. "I don't know, maybe," she says.

"Do you know where he's gonna be staying?" she asks.

"No, but hopefully with his father and not at the house," she adds.

"All right, well if you talk to him, tell him I said hey," Gia says, then walks away with her pizza slice and soda. She sits with another girl and two guys. I don't pay attention to her after that.

"She's looking for Darien. What about Terrence?" I ask.

"See, she does this shit every time. She tries to get with

both of them. They get mad with each other and shit starts. See, that's what I thought you were doing at first."

"Nah, no way, I learned my lesson with your brother..."

"Half brother," Ursula quickly corrects.

"I learned my lesson with your half brother. No offence, but I seriously don't need that drama anymore."

"Yeah, I hear you."

I take the next order and go back to work. An hour and a half later, it's about time to close. I'm tired now. It feels like I've been on my feet for days. Giorgio locks the doors, but there are still a few people left inside eating. Sierra, Ursula and I start cleaning up the front area. We have to make sure all the trays are off the tables and pick up any trash on the floor, so it can be mopped up later.

Behind the counter, we wipe everything down and put all the extra stuff like frozen fries and meat patties back in the freezer. Ursula is emptying out the soda tray and Sierra is helping scrape down the fry grill. I am putting the chairs up on the tables. The last customers leave, and the place is officially closed. Giorgio takes the two cash register drawers to his office, and the two cooks are cleaning the kitchen. When everything is clean and only the floor needs mopping, Giorgio tells me, Sierra and Ursula we can go home.

He walks us to the front door. Just when he unlocks and opens it to let us out, this guy comes over blocking us and talking about wanting to order a large pepperoni pizza to go. Giorgio tells him the restaurant is closed. The three of us keep walking out, and then these guys come out of nowhere and push us all back inside. Sierra and I fall to the floor and

Ursula is pushed up against the front window. It happens so fast, we have no idea what's even going on. Ursula hurries over and helps us up, and we just stand there as all four guys come inside. They lock the door again, then turn to us.

"Turn out the damn lights," one of the guys yells.

We just look at each other. The guy that yelled punches Giorgio in the face and tells him again to turn off the light. Giorgio stumbles back, holding his face. He hurries to the side to turn off the lights. "Look, man, just take the money, all of it. Just don't hurt us, okay?"

"Shut up, did I tell you to speak?" the same guy demands. Then he turns to the other three with him. They seem to be in shock watching this. "Go, what the hell are ya'll waiting for, go. Take care of the other two in back." The three other guys run to the kitchen. I could hear one of them yelling at the cooks in the kitchen to shut up and lay down on the floor. A few minutes later two of them come back to the front and nod to the third guy.

"All right, let's go to the back. Get one of them," he says, talking about us. He looks at me and grabs me first. Another guy grabs Sierra and the third guy grabs Ursula. We walk to the back of the restaurant. The guy that was doing all the talking grabs my hair and pulls me back so that we walk behind the other two. They line us up against the wall. Giorgio turns to say something and is punched in the face a second time as the guy yells at him to shut up again.

"Yo, chill out on that shit, man. That ain't right. You don't need to be doing all that," one of the guys says. He is holding Sierra's arm and they are standing right next to us.

"You shut up, too. I'm doing this. This is my thing. You just along for the ride, you crackhead punk. Remember that. You want to pay your debt, this is how you do it." On the other side Ursula struggles, and the guy grabs her harder. She screams and lurches back, nearly knocking him down and getting away. "Hold on to her," the guy holding me yells. I turn. The guy holding Sierra turns also to look at them and I see the ink on his neck.

Shit. All of a sudden I know that tattoo. The main guy has a fistful of my hair, but I can still see what is going on with Sierra and Ursula and the guys holding them. They all have dark ski masks on covering their faces and dark sunglasses over their eyes. Two of them act scared of the one guy holding me. "What the hell are you looking at, bitch? Turn around," he demands. I turn around fast. Then he leans over right in my ear. His hot breath is all over my neck. I cringe and close my eyes.

"You see something you want back here?" he whispers, snatching my hair harder, pulling me closer to his body. I feel like a rag doll being tossed around. He presses closer still. I feel like I am going to be sick. "You ain't got your pretty boy here to help you out now, do you? I can do whatever I want and you just have to take it."

"What you doing, man? Leave her alone, let's just get the money."

"Shut up. We got plenty of time. And all of a sudden, I feel like playing. What about it, pretty girl?" He snatches my hair again, "You want to play with me? You got all those other guys wrapped around your finger, but what you gonna do with a real man?"

I don't answer. I can't. I am too scared to breathe. The other three guys start yelling and complaining about messing around and not getting the money. The guy grabbing my hair tells them to shut up.

"Please, please, the money's in the cash register trays. Take it, just take it," Giorgio pleads. A second later, the guy's cell phone rings once. He doesn't answer, but seems to know what it means. "Shit," he yells really loud in my ear. "Let's go now. We gotta get out of here." We all hear sirens in the distance.

The two guys push Sierra and Ursula down, and the third guy comes running from the back. "What happened? Did ya'll get the money?" he says anxiously.

"Hell, no, he ain't get the money. Come on," one of the two guys yells, running to the front of the restaurant.

"Shit, I told him to stop playing around with her. We got nothing now. Check the cash drawers, quick."

"They're empty."

"What about the office?"

"It's too late, come on, we gotta get out of here."

"I told you to hurry up. I told you to hurry up."

"Shut up!"

They're all constantly yelling at each other in the front when the last guy is still holding on to my hair in back. "Come on, let's go," they yell to him.

"That means you, too, baby, let's go." He pulls me to the front of the restaurant like I am going with them. I seriously know that isn't going to happen. I am not going to be somebody's hostage. Just as he pulls me around the counter, I grab one of the pizza cutters and slash it across his hand. He screams and releases my hair. I don't look to see what damage I did. I just run as fast as I can to the back, knowing he is probably right behind me. "Forget her, man, come on," somebody yells. "Come on!"

As soon as I run to the back, Giorgio grabs me and pulls me into his office. He locks the door and stands against it. Ursula is already on the phone with the police, but they are on the way. Someone had already called. We hear someone call Giorgio's name. It's the cooks. They're okay. Giorgio opens the door and gets them inside with us. We are all just sitting on the floor in shock. Nobody says a word. Next we hear sirens close by, then there is a commotion up front. We all look at each other, afraid they've come back again. There is a loud bang on the door telling us to open up.

Giorgio unlocks the door, and the police barge in with guns drawn, nearly knocking him down. Sierra faints. I scream, and Ursula is yelling "No, no, no." They pull us out of the office one at a time, checking to see if we are armed or something. When they get to me, one of the cops yells to drop it. I have no idea what he is talking about. Two other cops come back to see what is going on. One cop pushes the other, yelling get out of the way. "Okay now, easy, put the knife down slowly."

I am just staring at him. He is talking and walks over to me slowly. "You're okay. You're okay. Give me the cutter."

I look at him and then at the pizza cutter in my shaking hand. It still has blood on it where I cut one of them. I drop it like it's a cobra about to strike. He kicks it away and another cop quickly snatches it up with some paper towels and jams it in a paper bag. "Are you hurt?" one of the cops asks me. I just look at him. "It's okay, it's over. Are you hurt?" I shake my head no. "Is that your blood on the pizza cutter?" he asks. I shake my head no again. "Did you cut one of them?" he asks. I nod. He smiles. "Good girl."

The next hour or so was a blur of craziness. There were cops everywhere and they were all talking and asking the same questions over and over again. Then these detectives came in and asked more questions. They questioned us separately and then together in a group. It was strange how we all had different perspectives as to what had happened. But we all agreed that it was two white guys and two black guys and the leader had me by the hair and he was going to take me with them.

Afterward, we each got a police escort home. I had the cop who got the cutter away from me. He explained to my grandmother what happened. She was furious when she found out. Of course I'm never allowed to work there again, or go there again or even eat pizza again. The cops stayed at our house until late. They were asking all kinds of questions, mostly about the break-ins in the neighborhood and then what I knew about Darien and his drama. I didn't say much. I didn't know much. I did know that tattoo. But I didn't tell them that.

CHAPTER 15

Something Familiar

"I've been asleep on a treadmill for so long that I can't remember what it feels like to be awake. I slow down just enough to look for the off switch, but I can't find it. I don't even know if there is one, but I'm still looking."
—*MySpace.com*

SUNDAY morning came down hard on me. I had nightmares the whole time and woke up in the middle of the night feeling like I was being strangled. I couldn't sleep in my bedroom on the third floor, so I went downstairs and stayed in my mom's old bedroom. It made me feel better, comforted, like I was connected to her again. I still had the nightmares, but at least I wasn't being strangled.

I woke up early, or rather, I didn't really sleep anymore, I don't know which one. Either way, my head was still splitting from that fool pulling on my hair. They say the whole thing only took fourteen minutes, but I swear it lasted a lifetime. Fast speed, normal speed or slow motion, I kept replaying it over and over again in my head. Nothing ever changed, it just kept happening. Every time I closed my eyes I heard them, smelled them, felt them. They're not around anymore, but they're still in my head.

Earlier, I jumped when I heard someone screaming. I was scared. I thought it was them coming back. But it was just someone outside playing around. The thing is, I can still hear them yelling to each other and the fool talking in my ear. It gives me the creeps to think he touched my hair like that. Now I just want to cut it all off and start over.

I asked my grandmother to cut it off last night, but she said no. She said cutting it would admit that he had something over me, and I was too strong a person to give in like that. She was right. Cutting it off would be the punk's way out. And I was no punk, so it stayed.

Dawn came and went and my grandmother didn't go to church, which was really amazing. She never misses church. So, I get up and shower for at least half an hour. I need to get the stench of that fool off my body and the smell of his breath off my neck. I just stay under the spray of water with my head down waiting to get clean from all this.

Afterward I get dressed and go back to my own bedroom. I sit at the windowsill looking down like I always do. I have a huge bay window with a cushioned seat, so I can see pretty far off around the neighborhood. I see Terrence's backyard, the top of Freeman Dance Studio and even The Penn. I am looking around trying to find familiar places, so I can get my world back to normal. But all of a sudden I have no idea what normal is anymore. The house phone's intercom system rings. There is a phone in the hall next to the back stairs. I pick up knowing who it is. "Yes, Grandmom," I say.

"Good morning, sweetie. Why don't you come on down and get yourself something to eat?"

"I'm not really hungry, Grandmom," I say.

"Of course you are, so come on down and eat. Do you feel like having some company?"

"Company?" I repeat. Then it hits me what she is talking about. "No, Grandmom, I don't want to see anybody today. Can you tell whoever it is that I'll catch up with them another time?" I say, hoping she isn't talking about her church friends or her bingo buddies. Don't get me wrong, the ladies are really nice, but I'm not in the mood to deal with them hovering over me all day.

"I'm sure you'll change your mind. Come on down and eat."

"Okay, can you turn the pantry light on for me?"

"Sure, come on down before breakfast gets cold."

I almost never use the back stairs. They lead to the pantry, and when the door is closed and the lights are out, it's creepy walking down into complete darkness. But since my grandmother turned the light on and opened the door, I'm cool. I go downstairs, and by the second floor landing I smell bacon and sausage cooking. My stomach grumbles. She was right. I am hungry.

As soon as I get to the pantry, I hear laughter. It's familiar. The kitchen door is cracked, and I open it all the way to see Jalisa at the stove turning the sausage links, Diamond pouring batter into the waffle iron and Jade pulling biscuits out of the oven. Damn, it is so good to see them. My grandmother is sitting at the kitchen table with the front page of the *Washington Post* in front of her, supervising. I walk into the kitchen smiling. It is the best company I could imagine. "What are ya'll doing here?" I ask happily.

"Girl, you know we had to come over after we heard about that craziness last night," Diamond says.

Jalisa nods. "I still can't believe it happened."

"Are you okay?" Jade asks.

I nod. "Yeah, I am now."

"All right, ladies, mind what you're doing. Watch the sausage and check the waffles. I smell something cooking too hard."

Jalisa immediately grabs the tongs, turns to the pan on the stove and rolls the sausage to check for doneness. Using the tongs, she pulls the sausages out and places them on the paper towel–lined platter beside the crispy bacon.

"Wow, everything smells so good," I say sitting down.

"Up you go," my grandmother says. "Grab some plates and silverware. Your job is to set the table. And don't forget the napkins."

I get up instantly and go to the top cabinets to get what I need to set the table. But I see that everybody is looking at my grandmother. I guess they thought she was going to take it easy and baby me or something. Wrong. That's definitely not her style. Actually, it feels pretty good to be around my family and friends doing something constructive together.

We eat brunch in the dining room 'cause we can't all fit around the kitchen table. The whole time I've been here, I don't ever remember eating in this room. First of all, it's enormous with a high ceiling and a major crystal chandelier. It has four huge windows that go from the floor all the way to the ceiling and some serious solid wood furniture. There is the table that seats ten people and the massive built-in side table and a china cabinet filled with the good stuff for special occasions. But there never are, so the special china just sits there. And it's funny that with all the fancy stuff in the room, the chairs are still covered with plastic.

We put the food on the table, then sit down to eat. Grandmom says grace, and we dig in like it's the last meal on earth. I can't believe how hungry I am. We talk and laugh as we eat. We tell Jade and my grandmother about LaVon's party Friday night. My grandmother tries not to laugh, but we know she is loving the story.

We talk about school. Jalisa and Diamond have funny stories about Hazelhurst, and I tell stories about being at The Penn. Then Jade talks about being at Penn Hall and now what it's like being in college. Then we start reminiscing about growing up and all the fun we used to have. That's when my grandmom starts telling us about what it was like when she was in school and what the neighborhood was like back then. It is actually interesting to hear the stories.

After breakfast, Grandmom says she'll clean the kitchen and tells us to go out and enjoy the day. Jade heads back to school because she has a big exam, and Jalisa, Diamond and I decide to go to Freeman to hang out.

"I didn't bring my dance stuff," Diamond says.

"Me, neither," Jalisa adds.

"You know what? I don't feel like dancing anyway. Why don't we go and just hang out?"

So that's what we do. We walk over. We pass Ursula's house and I wonder how she's doing. We decide to stop and see. Her mom answers the door and sends us up to her bedroom. I knock on the door, and she yells, "I'm busy."

"Ursula, it's me, Kenisha. Jalisa and Diamond are with me." I hear her hit the floor and walk to the door. She opens it and looks at me. "Hey, are you okay?" She doesn't say anything. "We're going to Freeman to hang out. Why don't you come with us?"

"I don't dance there. You know that."

"We're not going to dance. We're going to just hang out in one of the private rooms on the top floor."

"Nah, that's okay. I'll see you later," she says.

"Okay, we'll see you later," I say. We leave without saying anything more. When we get to Freeman, the door is open and Ms. Jay is just about to teach a beginner class. We ask for a key to one of the upstairs rooms. A few minutes later, we are just sitting on the floor talking, first about Friday night again, then about breakfast and then about Ursula. "Did she get hurt?"

"No, I don't think so," I say, trying to think if I remember her getting hit or something. "They pushed her into the front window."

"That whole thing must have been surreal," Diamond says.

"I can't even imagine going through something like that," Jalisa adds.

"It was crazy. It still feels like a dream."

"You mean a nightmare," Diamond corrects.

"I guess you're not going back there to work ever."

I shake my head, no. They both nod, agreeing with me. "You know there's always another pizza place around."

"I wanted to cut my hair off last night," I say quietly, completely changing the subject. Jalisa and Diamond look at me, questioning. "That's how he held me still and made me walk to the back with him. He grabbed and held my hair the whole time."

"That is so shitty. I hate that. I hate him."

"I know, right, bullies do shit like that and hide behind masks stealing money from people."

"Wait, ya'll heard about the ski masks, too. That part wasn't even on the news. How did ya'll find that out?" I ask.

"Li'l T," both Diamond and Jalisa say.

I shake my head and roll my eyes. "I should have known. That kid knows everything. Seriously, he's like super spy," I say.

"After we heard about it, we wanted to see you. Then your grandmother called my grandmother and asked if we could come over for the day," Diamond says.

I had no idea my grandmother asked them to come over. "I'm glad ya'll came. I feel so much better."

"Friends for life, girl," Jalisa adds. "That was the plan, right. We said it downstairs when we were four years old."

Diamond and I nod. That was our pledge. "Friends for life." I stick my hand out like they do on television. Diamond puts her hand on mine, and Jalisa puts her hand on Diamond's. We keep topping each other's hands until we fall over laughing. "Friends for life." Then, just as I say it, there is a knock on the door. We turn. Ursula peeks in the small glass window. She nods. We wave for her to come inside. She comes in and walks over to where we are sitting at the back of the room by the mirrors. "Hey, you came."

"Yeah, I didn't mean to interrupt. If this is private..."

"No," we all say.

"No, stay," Jalisa adds.

"Thanks." She sighs heavily and sits down on the polished hardwood floors with us. "I swear, I just couldn't stay home any longer. My mom was driving me crazy at home. She's hovering like a wet blanket. I can't breathe. Every time I open my bedroom door, she's there asking me if I'm okay or if I need anything. She must think I'm gonna explode or something."

We start laughing. She joins in.

"So, how are you doing?" I ask her.

"I still have a headache."

"Yeah, me, too," I say.

No one says anything for a while. Then out of the blue, we just start talking about homework, school, clothes, music, guys, sex, parents, food and anything else not related to what happened. Suddenly everything else fades into the background. After a while, we are all laughing like crazy at stories Ursula is telling us about when she was growing up. We get up and start showing Ursula some of our dance moves, and she even tries a few. She isn't bad at all.

We stay in the room for almost two and a half hours just talking about different things. When we finally leave, we walk Ursula back to her house, then Jalisa and Diamond come back to my house. My grandmother made brownies. We each grab one and go outside on the back step and eat.

I take a bite and say it. It was on my mind all day and I just have to get it out. "I think I know who one of the guys was who did it."

Jalisa and Diamond look at me. "What? Seriously?"

"Yeah, I think so," I say.

"You think so?" Diamond prompts.

"Are you sure?" Jalisa asks.

I shrug and half nod. "I wish I wasn't and I definitely wish I didn't see what I saw, but I did."

"Whoa, wait. How are you so sure about this? What did you see?"

I take a deep breath and release it slowly. "I can't tell you. Not because I don't want to, but I don't want you to get in any trouble. There were four guys there last night, one in the back with the two cooks, and the other three behind the counter with me, Sierra, Ursula and Giorgio."

"And..."

"They had us facing the wall. When the one who had my hair was yelling, I turned around and saw a tattoo on the other guy. I know that tattoo."

"Are you going to tell the police?"

"I can't," I say.

"What? Why not? 'Cause snitches get stitches?" Jalisa asks.

"Yeah, but he could have done anything and he's still out there," Diamond says. "Maybe you can do it anonymously."

"I can't because it would get someone I know in trouble."

My grandmother calls to me. We get up and go to the living room where she is. There are two men with her, one white and one black. "Kenisha, I'm Detective Clark and this is Detective Wilson. We'd just like to ask you a few more questions about last night." Then they look at Jalisa and Diamond.

"These are my girlfriends. They have to go anyway," I say. I turn and nod to both, and they nod back. I know they'd never say anything about what we talked about. We hug and they leave.

"Kenisha, come have a seat next to me," my grandmother says. I do. The police sit down on the chairs across from us.

"Kenisha, can you go over the story again, telling us exactly what you remember?"

I nod and tell them what happened. I still leave out the tattoo part. "Is there anything you remember at all about them?" one of the cops asks.

"Anything at all, maybe something so small you think it's not really important."

I shake my head and shrug. "They argued a lot."

"Really, tell us about that," the first cop says, writing this down. I tell them about Giorgio getting hit the second time and how one of the guys didn't like it. They both start writing. "Did they use any names or gang signs or anything else?"

"No. But I think the one grabbing my hair was the leader."

"Why do you think that?"

"He was the one ordering the others around. They seemed scared of him."

"What makes you say that?"

"Whenever he said something, they jumped and ran."

"Good, this is very good. Can you think of anything else?"

"No."

They stand up. "Okay, thank you for your time, Kenisha, Mrs. King. I know it's probably an inconvenience to come to you on a Sunday evening, but we like to talk to witnesses when things are fresh in their minds."

"We understand."

"If you can think of anything else, just give us a call." He hands me and my grandmother each a business card. "Good night."

My grandmother walks them to the front door while I stay in the living room for a while. She comes back a few minutes later. "Did you have a good day?" she asks.

I smile and nod. "Yes, I did. I didn't think I would this morning, but I'm glad I did."

"Good."

I get up to head upstairs. "Thanks for calling Diamond's grandmother."

She smiles knowingly. "You're welcome. Rest easy with pleasant dreams," she adds.

Unfortunately, that didn't happen.

CHAPTER 16

Was That Me?

"Screaming isn't an option, but I want to do it anyway. I hear myself in my head, screaming as loud as I can, but nobody else does. I'm screaming. I'm screaming. I'm screaming. Hey, wait a minute, I'm okay. Never mind."

—MySpace.com

The next day, Monday morning, I see Dr. Tubbs. He already knew what happened. My grandmother suggested I see him and then called him. I go just to see what he'll say. Surprisingly, today he isn't his usual reserved and blasé self. He's anxious and concerned. I've never seen him like this before. Of course, I've only been coming here for about a month or so.

We start out talking about school and me staying at Penn Hall. I tell him about my dad's money problems. He scribbles that down in his notebook quickly. Probably to make sure he sends the bill to him as soon as I leave. Then we talk about my family and friends and what's happening with me.

"Now tell me about what happened to you," he starts.

"The place I worked at got robbed."

"I'm sure there was more to it than that. How do you feel?"

"Tired of people asking me how I feel," I say, more like my old self. He nods and half smiles, I guess seeing the same thing. I am my old self still. "Yeah, I'm still the same smart-ass I was before, just with a lot more drama in my life."

"Yes, drama, you've had quite a bit of drama in your life lately. Just a few weeks ago with you and your friend in his room and then..."

I quickly interrupt. "No, *he* was definitely *not* my friend. His half sister is my friend and she hates him. We were kicking it for a while, but that's it. I thought you wrote all this stuff down. It looks like you're slipping," I challenge. He smiles again. I do, too. I think that's why I like coming here to see him sometimes. I can say whatever to him and it's all good. He doesn't care. In here, we're equals.

"I stand corrected. Tell me, do you feel put-upon?"

"Put-upon?" I repeat.

"It means targeted, victimized or exploited."

"Yeah, I know what it means. It's just so old and out-dated." I shake my head hopelessly. "Doc, seriously, you need to renew your subscription to *Ebony* and *Essence* magazines. Nobody says *put-upon* anymore." He chuckles this time. I swear, in all the times I've been coming to see him, this is the first time I've seen him even attempt to laugh.

"Perhaps you're right. Do you feel targeted?"

I think about it for a few seconds before answering.

He is right. There have been a lot of things going on in my life lately. Some I can control and some I can't. "You know what? No. I didn't feel victimized. I do feel unlucky sometimes."

We talk some more about general stuff going on in my life. Then we talk about me working again and not feeling the stress of being robbed again. "How do you feel about that?" he asks.

He's always asking me how I feel about something. But I'm getting used to it. "I feel like I need to get a better job next time," I joke.

"I need you to be serious this time, Kenisha. I don't want this very random experience to torpedo your desire to be self-sufficient."

"I know," I say seriously, "and don't think it has. I think I just need to find a job better suited for me anyway, maybe in retail or maybe dance."

He nods. "Good, excellent," he says with ease. "You sound good." He scribbles in his notebook.

"What are you looking for exactly?" I ask him.

He looks up at me. "I'm looking for signs that you're not coping with this situation well, particularly after the last situation with your *not*-friend."

"I know neither of the things that happened was my fault. Both times it was somebody else's stupidity interrupting my life."

He nods. "Exactly," he says, smiling wide this time. "You have an excellent grasp of reality. I wish some of my other patients were as clearly focused on discerning the ills of life as you are." He scribbles like crazy this time.

"I have a question for you. If I told you something, would you go tell the police with what I said? Would you tell?"

"If it would endanger you or someone else, I would be morally obligated to seriously consider it."

I roll my eyes. A simple yes or no would have done the trick. "So that's a yes, right?"

He doesn't respond. "Do you know something you should have told the police about the robbery?"

"If I do I'll get someone in trouble. In more trouble than they're already in."

"And if you don't they will be in even more trouble eventually?"

"No, I won't let that happen."

"You may not be able to prevent it."

I think about what he said for a minute. Maybe I can't prevent it or maybe I can. "I have another problem."

"Sure, go ahead. Tell me."

"I've been getting these phone calls from this girl."

"And…" he prompts.

I take a deep breath, 'cause all of a sudden it seems weird to talk to him about this. I look at him. He is watching me patiently, waiting for me to say something like he always does. "It's no big deal, really, it's just that she keeps calling and saying I have something and she wants it back."

"What does she think you have?"

"Money."

"I see. Do you indeed have her money?"

"No, no, definitely not. I have no idea what she's talking about. I don't have her money, I don't have *any* money. The only money I think I have is my mom's money and I can't get to that. Jade told me everything's set for college with mom's insurance policies, but that's it. I don't know what she's talking about."

"Did you tell her this?"

"She doesn't seem to be listening."

"Caller ID?" he asks. I shake my head. "Perhaps you should speak to your grandmother or father, whoever pays the phone bills. They can have the phone number blocked or have your phone number changed."

I nod, but I know that won't work in the real world. We finish up by talking about steps to be more aware of my surroundings at all times. We also talk about after-school programs that would be better use of my free time. I leave feeling great, and he promises to pick up a few *Essence* and *Ebony* magazines.

CHAPTER 17

Walking On the Wild Side

"I keep falling down and in the process all hell is breaking loose. I get that sometimes keeping quiet is better than screaming your head off. But forget what I said before, I really need to scream right now."

—*MySpace.com*

I skipped school the rest of Monday. I seriously didn't feel like going in. Hell, I wasn't sure I was ever going back to school again. Well, that's not true. I knew I had to go back to my life. I just wasn't ready to do it now. All I kept thinking was, damn, this is the second time something crazy like this happened to me. Okay, the last time I walked into it, but this time, I was minding my own business doing what I was supposed to be doing, and drama jumped up on me.

By the time Tuesday came and I got back to school, the attempted robbery at Giorgio's Pizza Place was old news. Everybody already knew about it, talked about it, was done with it. It was just like a hundred or so other robberies that go on in the hood. No big deal, old news. But what wasn't

old news were the rumors that the police had been to the
school again asking questions. They weren't gonna let this
go. Rumor now was that this attempted robbery was very
different from the other break-ins that had been going on
in the neighborhood.

So I'm sitting in my second period class trying to pay attention, and it's just not happening. It feels like everybody
is staring at me. And I know it's not just my imagination.
Then, later on, I find out why. Ursula texts me 'cause Sierra
texted her. Somebody told somebody that I was involved in
the robbery, and it was my "uppity crew" from my Virginia
private school coming in the hood doing it. *WTF.* The
rumor is flying around the school like wildfire. I'm sure by
noon everybody knows about it.

Okay, first of all, who the hell is in my "uppity crew"
and why the hell would anybody I know bother to rob
someplace around here? I know that might sound wrong,
but for real, if my friends were gonna rob someplace, they'd
definitely make it worth their while. So it was all BS started
by some idiot with nothing better to do than start some
drama. And yeah, I have a damn good idea who started the
shit—it was probably Cassie. It sounds just like something
she'd do.

After class I see Ursula at lunch. She walks over to me
just as I am leaving the food line. "Hey," she says.

I turn. "Hey, what's up? How you doing?"

"Please, girl, you don't even want to know. Did you hear
the shit going on with all this?"

"About my so-called 'uppity crew'?" I ask.

"Oh, hell, no, see that was this morning's rumor. This

afternoon's drama is that you were all hooked up in it because you need the money to go back to your private school."

I laugh. "And robbing a corner pizza place was gonna get me there. Obviously whoever started the rumor doesn't have a clue about how expensive Hazelhurst costs per semester. Believe me, I'd have to rob damn near every place around the way to even send them the first down payment," I say, just as Sierra comes over. It is the first time I've seen her since she passed out in Giorgio's office when the police came in with their guns drawn.

"Hey, ya'll talking about how Kenisha masterminded the whole thing 'cause she wants to take over the world?" We laugh because it is just that stupid. As scared as we all were at the time, nobody in their right mind could say anything so stupid. We know the truth and that's what matters. "But you okay?" she asks me.

I nod. This is weird. This is the same person who barely speaks to me. And yeah, this is the same person who was in my face about Troy at my locker just a few days ago. "Yeah, I'm okay. What about you? Are you okay?"

She nods. "I still have headaches and nightmares."

"Yeah, me, too," both Ursula and I say.

"They said your face was all cut up and you were having plastic surgery in the hospital yesterday," Sierra says.

I shake my head. This place is like rumor city on crack. Every five minutes there's something new and something just as stupid. It is ridiculous because pretty much nobody has brains enough to question if the rumors even make any sense. "No, I just didn't feel like coming to school yesterday."

"I wish I'd stayed home, but my mom was driving me crazy all weekend," Ursula says.

"The only reason I came yesterday is I didn't want to be in the house by myself," Sierra admits.

We keep talking. I drink my drink, but none of us really eats our lunch. We just push the food around on our plates until the bell rings, then we go our separate ways. It is the last class of the day. For me, it is U.S. History and Ms. Grayson. Since my locker is on the way to her class, I make a quick stop. I definitely don't want to run into Troy and his crew today.

I walk into the class just before the late bell rings. Ms. Grayson closes the door as soon as I walk in. "Okay, okay, people, let's settle down. We have a lot to do, so let's get started." Since we have assigned seats and every seat is taken, it is easy to see no one is absent from her class. She glances around the room quickly, then walks over to her desk. The first thing Ms. Grayson usually does is do an extra credit current event thing. All we have to do is bring in a newspaper clipping about a current event so the class can talk about it. "All right, anybody want to do a current event?"

Nobody ever does this except for right before report card grades go in or when we are having a quiz and we want to take up most of class time, so we don't have time for the quiz. But today someone volunteers. Everybody turns around, including me. Cassie has her hand up.

"Cassie, are you volunteering?" Ms. Grayson asks.

"Yeah," she says, pulling out her newspaper clipping.

"My current event is the robbery at Giorgio's Pizza Place last Saturday. I have the newspaper, and it says here that the police think it was an inside job," she says, and then looks directly at me. Thirty-seven pairs of eyes turn to look at me, too. "So obviously somebody, I'm not saying who, did it."

"You just like to hear yourself talking, don't you?" I say.

"All right, all right," Ms. Grayson says, while clapping her hands. She tries to regain control of her class, but nobody pays any attention to her. "All right, that's enough, Cassie. You're finished. And don't even pretend to think you're getting extra credit for that."

"She knows she did it or she's covering up protecting someone who did," Cassie says accusingly.

"Vous est une telle chienne," I mutter under my breath, but loud enough for her to hear me, but not knowing I'd just said she was such a bitch.

"Kenisha," Ms. Grayson says quickly, "this isn't French class. Watch your language. Some of us speak French very well."

"What did you say about me, skank?" Cassie asks.

"Cassie, watch your language, too," Ms. Grayson says.

"See, that's why nobody likes your ass now. You think you're so much better than everybody else here."

"Actually, I don't, but obviously you have a problem. You know what? Seriously, you need to get yourself a hobby and get up off my ass."

Everybody starts laughing.

"Skank," she says.

"*Chienne,*" I say, calling her a bitch in French again.

"That's it, both of you outside," Ms. Grayson demands. Neither one of us moves an inch.

"Who are your four friends, Kenisha?" she taunts.

"I said that's enough, Cassie," Ms. Grayson says louder.

I open my mouth to respond, but then it hits me. I start laughing, and everybody looks at me. "Oh, my God, it was you, wasn't it?"

"It was me what?" she says, quickly wondering what I am talking about.

"Both of you get up," Ms. Grayson says. Neither one of us still moves. The whole class is out of control by this time. Everyone is talking and laughing and pointing fingers.

"It was you," I say again. Cassie just looks at me this time. Her eyes get wide as she stares. "See, nobody knew how many were there Saturday night except the people in the restaurant. You weren't in the restaurant and you're not a cop, so tell me, Cassie, how do you know exactly how many there were?"

"What?" she says, as everybody looks at her now. "I just guessed, no, I saw it in the newspaper."

I shake my head no. "No, it wasn't in the newspaper. That's one of the things the police wanted us not to talk about. So, how did you know if you weren't involved?"

"It wasn't me," she screams.

"It was you. You're the one, or maybe you were just too high to remember, just like with Darien," I say again, as I turn it all back on her and am liking the fact that she is getting all freaked out about it now. But actually I am just bluffing. The police didn't tell us that, and I have no idea what was in the newspaper, since I made a point of not reading it.

"That's it. Enough, get up," Ms. Grayson demands, standing directly in front of me. "Over to the door, now."

"No," Cassie repeats. "It wasn't me, it was you."

I get up and walk to the door, shaking my head. I am too calm and composed. "It was you, that's why you're trying to blame somebody else. It's reverse psychology. That's why you start all the rumors, so nobody looks at you to see the truth."

"Get up, Cassie, right now."

She finally gets up, and by this time, she is in near hysterics. Just as we are going outside, the classroom phone rings. "Sit down," Ms. Grayson commands to the rest of the class who had basically gotten up to follow and see what was going to happen. "You two stay right there and shut up."

She goes to the front of the class and answers the phone. She looks at me, nods and agrees, then hangs up. "Kenisha, you're wanted in the main office. Go."

"Probably the police to lock your ass up," Cassie says.

"You stand right there because you're going to detention."

"For what? Reading the newspaper and telling the truth?" she yells. "That's not right."

I smile and stick my tongue out childishly as I walk out. Most of the class starts laughing. Cassie starts bitching. I leave feeling pretty good. Once I get outside, it occurs to me I was summoned to the main office. I have no idea what that means. So I am walking down the empty hall and I hear my name called. "Hey, Kenisha. Kenisha." I turn around seeing Li'l T running up behind me. "I was trying to text you. Your phone's been off all day," he says.

"Yeah, I know. I leave it off mostly now," I say.

"Well, you need to turn it back on sometimes."

I don't need a lecture from Li'l T right now. "What's up?"

"Nothing much. What was all that about?" he asks.

I glance back at the classroom door. It is still closed. "It's just Cassie drama. Her fifteen minutes of fame are definitely up. She needs to disappear now."

He starts laughing. "Yeah, I like that. She always trying to play somebody. But yo, you okay about what happened?"

"Yeah, I will be," I say, getting tired of people asking.

"Man, when I saw those guys push ya'll in the restaurant and punch Gio in the face, I damn near passed out. I swear I knew they was gonna make a move," he says anxiously.

I stop walking. "Wait, what do you mean, you knew they were going to make a move? Did you have something to do with what happened?"

"Nah. Nah. How you even gonna play me with that? Nah, I saw them sitting in a car out front. So I walked by and was eyeing this one guy in the backseat 'cause he was eyeing me, too. Then this other dude jumped in my face talkin' 'bout he's gonna kick my ass if I don't get out of there."

"Why didn't you call the police if you knew this?" I say, looking at him all pissed off.

"I did. They said sitting in a car wasn't against the law. So then I just waited around across the street where they couldn't see me. When I saw Gio walking you to the door and that one guy get out, I knew there was gonna be trouble. I ran to the gas station and called the police on the pay phone. You know it took them forever just to answer the phone and when they did they wanted all this information. I called the fire department just to get somebody down there. It still took the police forever to get there."

"We called from the office after they left. They said the police were already on the way. So it was you who called first."

"Yeah, but it didn't help much."

"Did you see their faces?" I ask.

"No, just the one guy in the backseat," he says, and then looks at me knowingly.

"You know who it was, don't you?" He nods. "It was the guy with the tattoo on his neck." He nods again. "Yeah, me, too. You gonna tell the police?" I ask. He shakes his head, no. I nod. "Me, neither. I gotta go," I say, looking around the empty hall.

"Yeah, me, too," he says. "But one more thing," he says solemnly. My stomach jumps. I swear I know exactly what he is gonna say even before he says it. "He's out."

I stop walking again. He doesn't have to say anything more than that. I know exactly who he is talking about.

"I just saw Ursula today at lunch. She didn't say anything," I say.

"She probably doesn't know. He got out of county jail yesterday. He's at his dad's house in Maryland."

"House arrest?" I ask hopefully.

He shrugs. "I don't know. I guess so."

"So if it's house arrest, he can't leave his father's house, right? The ankle bracelet won't let him, right?"

"You know there's ways of getting around everything."

We get to the office. "I gotta go in," I say.

"See you later," he says and keeps walking.

As soon as I get in the main lobby area, I see that same idiot woman sitting at the desk. As usual, she is on the phone talking and laughing about something. "My name is…" I begin, but she holds her skinny finger up. I roll my eyes and wait. This is so ridiculous. She keeps talking on the phone basically ignoring me. So I walk away and head to the next desk.

"Hey, hey, hey, get back here. You can't go in there!"

"As I was saying, my name is…"

"I said, wait a minute. Just be quiet and have a seat. As soon as I'm done, I'll get to you."

Just as she says that, one of the vice principals comes out of his office and walks over. The idiot behind the desk hangs up instantly. "I asked for Kenisha Lewis to come to the office. Where is she?" he asks.

"I'll call the class again," the idiot says. Of course I'm sitting right here hearing and seeing all this. I let her call. A few minutes later the vice principal comes out again. This time he looks at me and walks over.

"What are you doing here?" he asks gruffly.

"The receptionist told me to sit down and be quiet."

He makes a quizzical face. "Kenisha Lewis," he says. I nod. "Go inside." He points to his office. I get up and start walking. He follows, but stops at the reception desk.

The idiot receptionist is just getting off the phone again.

"Ms. Grayson said she was sent here five minutes ago. Maybe she left the school."

"Or maybe Kenisha Lewis has been sitting right there waiting for you to send her into my office."

"But I didn't know..."

That's all I hear as I walk into the vice principal's office and see my father sitting in one of the chairs. He stands as soon as I walk in. "Baby girl, are you okay?" he asks.

"Yeah, fine," I say trying to figure out why he's here.

The vice principal comes in a few seconds later. My dad meets him midway in the office and shakes his hand. "Thank you." Okay, I'm just standing there looking lost, 'cause I have no idea what's going on. "Come on, Kenisha, you're signed out. Let's go."

Okay. Whatever. I follow my dad out of the building and to his car. This is so familiar. I so remember doing this after my fight with Regan about a month ago. As soon as we get in the car, he starts. "Why the hell didn't you tell me what happened to you?"

"Hi, Dad," I say drily.

"Don't 'hi, Dad' me. You're not working at that pizza parlor anymore. So what the hell is going on?"

"Excuse me?"

"Don't hand me that 'excuse me' bullshit. You heard me. What the hell is going on? This afternoon I get in the office and everybody is asking me how my daughter's doing after what happened over the weekend. Then a few minutes later two detectives come into my office and tell me my daughter was in an attempted robbery at her job. Imagine that. I didn't even know about it. Do you know how stupid I felt

not knowing anything going on in my own household?"
Okay, I don't say anything 'cause duh, I already know this
part. "Answer me," he yells.

Okay, my dad never yells at me, so this is getting crazy.
"I'm sorry if what happened to me over the weekend while
you were in New York messed up your day or embarrassed
you at the office."

"What the hell is that supposed to mean?" he asks.
I assume it is rhetorical so I don't say anything again.
"Well…" he prompts for a reply. My bad, not rhetorical. I
shrug. "No, you're not getting off that easily. What the hell
happened?"

"The detectives told you, right?" I say. He glances over
and glares at me. I can see he is furious now all of a sudden.
Fine, I need to expound. "I was working and the place got
robbed."

"Since when are you working?"

"Since I found out you don't have any money."

"So you think some stupid-ass little pizza job gonna get
your ass back in Hazelhurst?"

"No, but I think it's gonna help out around the house
where I live."

"Not anymore. You're moving back to the house."

"What house?" I ask, totally surprised by this.

"The Virginia house," he says.

"No," I nearly scream. My heart slams in my chest.

"What do you mean, no? I'm still your father and I'm the
only one determining where you live and go to school. This
is the second time in almost as many weeks that something

dangerous has happened to you. You're moving back to Virginia."

"I thought you were selling the house," I say.

"Not anymore, that's off," he says.

"I guess New York worked out for you then."

He doesn't say anything, but I see his jaw tighten and a muscle in his neck pull hard as he grimaces in profile. There is no way he was in New York last weekend, and I bet his business is just fine.

We don't say anything to each other the rest of the way to the house in Virginia. Then as soon as we pull up in the driveway, I see this beat-up old car parked in front of the house. "You have company," I say.

"What the hell is this?" he mutters, and this time I know it is rhetorical.

We get out of the car and go to the front door. He opens it, and I walk in first. He comes in, leaving the door wide open. Neither one of us says anything as we look around. I get my cell phone out just in case something is about to jump off and I need to call for help quickly. Then we hear muttering and talking coming from his office. I follow him as he heads in that direction. The office door is open and we walk in.

Courtney is there with a man. She is half sitting on the desk, and the man is in my dad's chair. They are both intent on looking at his computer monitor. They don't look up or see us come in. Again, neither me nor my dad says a word. I look at him. I swear if he was a cartoon character his face would be beet red and stacks of steam would be coming out of his ears. Yeah, he looks that mad.

I quickly turn on the camera video application on my cell phone and point it at them. Courtney and the guy are talking, but at first we can't hear what they're saying. Then they start talking louder. This is like the most outrageous thing I've ever seen and I'm getting every second of it on video.

"*...you see right now it doesn't show a lot,*" the man says.

"*But I know he's got money. He just won't give it to me. I hate this shit and I'm not getting dumped without a penny...*"

OMG, please tell me this is not what I think it is. I make sure to aim the cell phone to get everything going on.

"*...you'll get child support.*"

"*...for three kids, what the hell is that? No, hell no, I want more than a couple hundred dollars a month. That's bullshit. Whatever bitch he has now is probably already pregnant, just like I was. I know how to play that game.*"

Never mind, it is exactly what I think it is. Courtney and whoever this man is are plotting on my dad and his money. And OMG, he's standing right here.

"*...well, this isn't showing anything,*" he says with his eyes still glued to the monitor.

"*Maybe he has another set of books like they do on TV.*"

"*Or maybe another file, but you'd have to find it...*"

"*I bet it's at his office, I could check there,*" she says. "*He's there now, so I'll do it later this afternoon. He never works past three o'clock. I'll go in then and look around.*"

The man nods. "*All right, so if that's the case, I think your best bet is to file as soon as possible before he moves any major assets. If he finds out you're doing this, it might get very ugly...*"

"*He can't do shit to me or I'll take the boys.*"

"Don't underestimate him," the man says, placing his hand on her knee and rubbing up her thigh under her short skirt.

"Look, at this point I just want what I deserve. I want half of everything."

"Realistically, you can't get half. You're not married."

"We've been together for over five years. Isn't that called common-law marriage?"

"No, Virginia doesn't recognize common-law marriage. And besides, you weren't living together all that time. And he wasn't with you exclusively."

Okay, I swear I want to pee my pants right now. This is straight-up some stupid dumb stuff you see in the movies. I'm like duh, idiots, look up. Candid friggin' camera. America's funniest friggin' home videos. Look up. We're standing right here. Hell, he's standing right here. But of course I'm not saying anything. I just want to see their faces when they do finally look up. I swear I am ready to explode.

Then it happens. He looks up first as he gets ready to stand up. He winces, but doesn't say anything. His jaw drops and he makes a gurgling sound as he jumps back in the chair. Courtney looks at him. "What the hell is wrong with you?" she asks, and then turns around.

Oh, man, it is *b-e-a-u-t-i-f-u-l*. I couldn't have asked for a more perfect expression. To say she is shocked wouldn't even come near to what her expression is. She like yelps and jumps and falls off the side of the desk. I swear the whole room shakes when she goes down on her ass. That has to hurt. I try my best to laugh quietly, 'cause I am still videotaping all this. But my hand starts shaking 'cause I am laughing so hard inside. Tears are rolling down my face, but I know I have to be quiet to keep videotaping. "Busted," I say quietly.

Her hand comes up first. Then she peeks up over the side of the desk like she is five years old. She stands up and shakes her head. I look at my dad. He still isn't saying anything. But now his fists are tight and the muscle or vein in the side of his neck is almost sticking straight out.

"Baby, I'm glad you're home. This isn't what you think. I swear. It wasn't me. He made me do it. He wanted the money, not me. I just want our life together."

The guy's jaw drops almost to the carpet. "What the hell—you bitch. Nah, nah, look, look, look, sir, I'm an attorney," he quickly fumbles and grabs a crinkled card from his shirt pocket. His hand shakes the whole time. "Your, ah, friend here hired me to go through your finances..."

"He's lying, James. I didn't hire him," Courtney screams, and then she instantly softens as she comes around the front of the desk. "You know I love you, baby. It's me and you, remember?"

My dad looks at the attorney guy. "Get out. Don't ever let me see you again," he says, menacingly. The man scrambles to his feet and grabs his beat-up briefcase. He's stumbling a couple of times when he has to walk around my dad and me since we are still standing near the open doorway. A few seconds later, he's gone.

I start laughing and waiting for my dad to blow up at her now. But to my surprise, he never really does. He doesn't even kick her ass out like he did me and my mom. I look at my dad's face, wondering what he's thinking. He has this dark smirk going on. Okay, this is new. I've never seen this expression before.

I finally turn off the video recorder on my cell phone.

Beautiful.

CHAPTER 18

Only One Logical Conclusion

"When you're in a hole, here's the friggin' thing, stop diggin'. Don't you know the deeper you go the harder it's gonna be to get out."

—Twitter.com

SO, now I'm on the flip side of all that. I'm in my room still laughing my ass off every time I think about what happened downstairs. Plus, I still have the video. My door is open, so I can hear Courtney begging and groveling about how she's in postpartum and her hormones are making her do crazy things. My dad still isn't saying much. Every once in a while he just says that he doesn't want to hear it.

"...James, please talk to me, please. I said I was sorry to let some ambulance-chasing wannabe lawyer come into our happy home and sabotage what we have together..."

Okay, this is the part where I usually put in my earbuds or turn my music up real loud, but I want to know what is going to happen. My dad was so mad when we walked in there and heard them talking. I thought he might try and kill the guy. And I know that guy was scared to death. As an ex-football player, my dad's pretty strong and muscled. The skinny lawyer guy shook the whole time I was there. But all in all, my dad was cool about it. He told the guy to get out of his house and that he never wanted to see him ever again. The man ran. And I'm not talking about hurrying up or walking quickly. No, when I say he ran, I seriously mean it. He shot out of there like his butt was on fire.

"...see, if you would just have been with me last weekend none of this would have happened. I'm not saying it was your fault what happened, but I would have felt so much better having you here with me. James, talk to me..."

Okay, I close my door, enough of the pleading. I call my grandmother at the house but don't get an answer. I figure she is still out at the senior citizen's center. That's another place she likes to go. Seriously, for an old woman who doesn't work, she has a hundred places to go and a million things to do to fill up her time. Today is senior center and then bingo. I end the call and am just about to call Jalisa when my cell rings. I answer, not thinking. "Hello?"

There is no answer at first, then I hear talking in the background, and I figure it's the private caller again. I end the call immediately just as someone says my name. I turn my phone off. I hate this. I get up to talk to my dad about the calls. I walk down the hall to what used to be my mom and dad's bedroom. The door is open. My dad is sitting in his armchair watching television with a glass of something in his hand. There is a college basketball game on.

I knock and go in. Courtney turns and glares up at me.

Looks like I am the one she's pissed at now. "We're busy," she snaps.

"Dad," I begin, ignoring her.

"Kenisha, I said we were busy right now. You need to come back later."

"I'm not here to talk to you, Courtney. Dad…"

"Kenisha, give me a minute," he says, still watching TV.

I nod. "Okay, fine," I say. I turn to leave and then he calls me back. I turn to him again.

"Wait, what do you want?" he asks.

"I need to talk to you about my cell phone."

"Your cell phone," Courtney repeats. "I can't believe you. This world does not revolve around you, Miss Kenisha. If you want another cell phone, get a job and buy one."

"I had a job," I say quickly.

"Then get another one," she adds, just as quickly.

"All right, enough," my dad says. "Kenisha, you're not getting a new phone. There's nothing wrong with the one you have."

"If you'd hear me out and not just jump on what she says, you'd know that I don't want or need a new phone."

"Well, then, what do you want?" Courtney asks, impatiently.

My dad looks at me blankly. I can see he isn't going to be much help, so forget him. I'll take care of this by myself. I am getting used to doing my own thing. Why stop and ask for help now? "You know what? Never mind," I say turning and leaving.

"Kenisha," I hear my dad call my name. I just keep

walking. Seriously, I don't need this. Then just as I close my bedroom door, I hear the front door open and loud giggling. Then there is running up the stairs. I hear the boys running down the hall calling for our dad. They sing a "dad's home" song over and over again. I grab my backpack off my bed to leave. Then it hits me. I need a ride to the Metro station.

I grab my phone from the backpack. The little white message light is blinking. I look at it. I'm sure it is just another missed call from "Private Caller." I sit on the side of the bed scrolling through all the messages I missed in the past few days. The last message was from Diamond just two minutes ago. I call her back.

"Hey, guess what?" I say, as soon as Diamond picks up.

"Where are you? What's wrong with your phone?" Diamond asks. "It's Kenisha," I hear her say to someone she is with.

"What? Nothing," I say.

"Jalisa, Jade and I have been trying to call you all afternoon. Your neighbor called the police. Somebody broke into your grandmother's house. Li'l T told us they trashed your room and Jade's room."

"What?" I scream. "Oh, my God, what about my grandmother?"

"She's fine. She wasn't home when they were there. Where are you?"

"In Virginia," I say. "Can you give me a ride?"

"My mom has her car," she says sadly.

"Don't worry about it," I say. "I'll call a cab home."

"No, Jalisa just said Natalie can give us a ride to D.C.," Diamond says.

"Okay. I'll meet you at Jalisa's house."

"Why don't we just meet you at your dad's?"

"No, I gotta get out of here. I can't stay," I say. Just then my bedroom door bursts open. My dad is standing in the doorway looking at me like he is all pissed and concerned. Oh, please. "I'll see you in a few minutes." I close my cell and stuff it in my book bag.

"What's wrong with you?" he asks.

"Nothing," I say.

"If nothing's wrong, then why did you scream?" he asks.

"Nothing," I say again.

"Kenisha's home. Kenisha's home." The boys are singing.

"Come back in here," I hear Courtney yelling.

A few seconds later the boys come peeking around my dad's legs, still calling my name. "Kenisha. Kenisha. Kenisha."

"Get back in here," Courtney yells again. She is louder this time. She must have been coming down the hall to my bedroom because the boys made a mad dash to my bed. They hop on and grab me. I give them a big hug just as Courtney rams up behind my dad still in the doorway. "Go to your room," she demands. They don't move and I hold tight.

"Jr., Jason, let's go," Dad says. The boys climb down slowly and walk to our dad. They turn to me. I smile and wave. They wave back. Then they run to get away from

Courtney. My heart sinks, thinking she'll catch them. Then I hear them yelling again. "Cash. Cash. Cash. Cash."

"Come on in here, little guys," Cash says from the door down the hallway. Fine, I know they'll be okay now.

"Kenisha…" my dad begins again.

I stand up and grab my bag. "I gotta go," I say, trying to brush pass him. He steps over and blocks my exit. "No, I said you're staying here, didn't I?"

Oh, please, does he really think he's gonna do this with me? "Dad, I gotta go now."

"What's going on?" he asks again.

"Nothing you would be concerned about."

"You're grounded. You're in your room for the rest of the night," he says, trying to act all parental for the first time in his life.

Seriously, I try not to laugh. I nod and stomp back to the bed and plop down playing the pissed off teenager. He must have thought he succeeded, 'cause he leaves and closes the door behind him. "And the Oscar goes to…" I whisper happily. I swear, I almost can't stop smiling. When my mom was alive and he was "at work" all weekend, I'd sneak in and out of the house on a regular basis. I get up, lock the bedroom door and open the window and roll my eyes. This is almost too easy.

I get to Jalisa's house in no time. They are already standing outside waiting for me. We drive to D.C. A block away from my grandmother's house, we see the police car still parked out front. There are a few people standing around looking. Natalie parks down the street and we run to the house. I bust in looking for my grandmother. "Grandmom," I yell.

"In here," she says.

She is in the kitchen. I run to her and grab her. "Are you okay?" I ask.

"Fine," she says. "Are you okay?"

"Yeah, fine. We got robbed?" I ask.

She nods. "Jade is upstairs going through her bedroom now. The detectives want you to do the same thing."

"Okay," I say, then I look at her again. "Are you sure you're okay?" I ask again. She nods and smiles.

I take the back stairs to my bedroom. Jalisa and Diamond follow, Natalie stays with my grandmother. When we get to my bedroom, I am stunned. "Shit, what the hell?"

"Kenisha."

I run out of my bedroom and meet Jade halfway down the hall. We hug like we used to, like sisters. "Are you okay?" we both ask at the same time. Then we smile and nod. "Good," she says. One of the detectives that was at our house Sunday night comes out of her room.

"Kenisha," he says, "I'm Detective Clark. I was here last Sunday evening..."

I nod. "Yeah, I know. I remember you," I say.

"Good. I'm gonna need you to try and look around your bedroom and see if anything's missing. We've already taken pictures and dusted, but I doubt we'll find any useable prints."

I look at Jade. This is all so crazy. "Does the rest of the house look like this?" I ask.

"No," Jade says. "Just our bedrooms."

"What? Why?" I ask.

"I'd say the thief or thieves were looking for something specific from either one or both of you."

"This is so sick," I say, going back in my bedroom and looking around at the disaster.

"We'll help you clean it up. Don't worry," Jalisa says. Diamond nods.

"Your friend Ursula's house was trashed, too," Jade says. "I tried to call you. What's wrong with your cell phone?"

"Nothing. I keep it turned off. I keep getting crank calls."

"What kind of crank calls?" Detective Clark asks.

"Some girl keeps calling saying she wants her money back. But I don't have her money. I don't know what she's talking about."

"Wait here," the detective says, then hurries downstairs. A few minutes later, he comes back with his partner, Detective Wilson. "Please tell Detective Wilson what you just told me."

"What—you mean about the crank calls?" I ask. He nods. I repeat what I just said.

"Your friend Ursula mentioned crank calls they've been getting at her house, too. She also mentioned that someone had been at their house before.

"Oh, my God," I say.

"What?" the detective asks.

"One time I came home and the back door was unlocked. Then another time it was just barely closed. Then last week, I don't remember when, I was up here in my bedroom and I heard the first floor steps creak. You know how they do,"

I say to Jade. She nods. "So when I leaned over the railing up here in the hallway and called down to my grandmother, thinking it was her, all I heard was a kind of shuffle and then the door close."

"What happened then?" Jade asks.

I shrug. "I went downstairs just as Grandmom was coming in the front door. I figured she made two trips with her bags. But then she only had one grocery bag."

Both detectives write everything down. "Do you have any idea what you and Ursula have in common, classes at school, teachers, friends, enemies?"

"Darien." It's like a chorus of four. Jade, Diamond, Jalisa and I all say his name at the same time.

"Darien Moore?" We all nod. "Bingo," Detective Clark says. "That's our common denominator. Did he give you anything to hold for him, maybe a bag or some luggage or a box?"

I look at him and crinkle my face. "No, never," I say.

Just then Terrence comes running upstairs two at a time. We all turn and look at him. I go deathly still and look at the two cops. He hurries past everyone and grabs me. We hug. Damn this feels good, but still I know he can't be here. When he finally releases me, he looks at me hard. "Are you okay?" he asks.

"Yeah," I whisper, "but what are you doing here?"

He looks at me strangely. "I heard about what happened. Li'l T called me."

"He what?" I say, getting pissed off all over again. I can't believe Li'l T would get Terrence here knowing the police were still walking around. I swear I'll kill that fool.

"Uh, okay, Kenisha," Detective Clark says, "we're gonna need you to look around in your room. See if you can tell if anything is missing. We'll be downstairs."

"Yeah, I'm a go, too," Jade says. "There's nothing missing in my bedroom that I can tell."

"We'll be downstairs, too," Diamond says. Jalisa nods and follows.

As soon as they leave I grab Terrence's hand and drag him inside. I wince again when I see my room. Everything has been trashed and my clothes are tossed everywhere. All my books on my bookshelves are knocked down, and my bed, desk and dresser are turned upside down. "What are you doing here?" I ask again. "You know how dangerous it is for you to be here with them still walking around. Are you crazy?"

"What are you talking about?" he asks.

"You know exactly what I'm talking about," I say as quietly as possible. "The thing, the other night." He looks at me completely puzzled. "Come on, I know all about it. I saw you and I know you saw me."

"Kenisha, did you hit your head or something? The last time I saw you was at the funeral last week."

"No, Saturday night," I mouth, fearful the police are around.

"What are you talking about?" he asks again.

I go to my bedroom door, look down the hall and stairway and then close it quietly. I pull him into the closet. "The robbery. I saw you, your tattoo."

"You saw my tattoo?" he repeats. "Which tattoo—this

one?" he says, pointing to his neck. I nod. "And you think I was there robbing the place." I nod.

"Don't worry, nobody knows. I would never say a word. I'll take it to the grave. I just need you to promise me that you'll never do anything like that again. I know we've been having our problems, but if you need money, maybe I can ask my sister again."

"Whoa, whoa, whoa, wait, hold up. You seriously think it was me the other night who attacked you."

"I saw you," I say. I reach up to touch the tattoo on his neck.

He backs off, leaning away from me. "Girl, you trippin', you actually think that was me. You really don't know me, do you?"

"I don't know why you're getting all pissed off. I'm just trying to protect you."

"Yeah, by thinking I'm some kind of street thug that goes around stealing and robbing people."

"It wasn't just me. Li'l T saw you, too."

"What?" he says loudly.

"Yeah, Li'l T."

"I don't care what Li'l T said he saw."

"We talked about it. He saw the car and one of the guys who got out and pushed us all back inside."

"I don't know who you think you saw, but it wasn't me."

"Terrence…"

"I don't want to do this," he says. "Why don't you just look around your room like the police asked you?"

I look around my bedroom seeing everything I guess was

there. I really can't tell. There is just too much stuff around all over the place. "Can you tell if something's missing?" he asks coldly.

I shrug. "I don't know." I look around again. It's no use. I don't have a clue.

"What about your jewelry?"

"Oh, my God, my mom's jewelry. I forgot about that." I run into our bathroom and check where I keep my jewelry. Like Jade suggested when I first moved in, I keep it where she keeps hers, in the bottom vanity drawer were we dump tampons and pads. That drawer wasn't even touched. All the jewelry is still there. I feel relieved for the first time that night. "Come on," I say, "I don't want to do this anymore, either."

He nods. We go downstairs and find everybody in the living room. My grandmother is telling one of her "I remember when" family stories about my great-great aunt who traveled all over the world and made a fortune. Everybody is sitting and standing around listening like she was imparting the knowledge of the universe. Maybe she is. She has a way of doing that sometimes. Terrence and I stand in the open doorway next to Jade listening, too.

Just as she finishes her story, the doorbell rings like crazy. The cops quickly look at each other and then nod. We are all trying to figure out what that means when the bell starts ringing like crazy again. "I'll get it," Jade says, heading to the door.

"No," Detective Wilson says. Clark nods and goes to the door. He opens it.

"Who the hell are you?" I hear my dad demand. *Shit. I forgot all about him.* "Where's my daughter?"

Detective Clark flips out his badge and introduces himself. "What's going on?" my dad asks, changing his tone instantly. He rushes in, seeing Jade first. "Jade, what's going on, is your grandmother okay? Is Kenisha here?"

I roll my eyes. This is going to be a long night.

CHAPTER 19

Now What?

"Am I maturing? Am I growing up? I don't know. Maybe I'm just tired of holding on to the old me? Still, growing up, this blows. When you know you're going to fail a test, why even bother taking it?"

—*MySpace.com*

The next three days were uneventful. Absolutely nothing happened. It felt strange not to have to duck and dodge drama for a few minutes. Cassie hadn't spoken to me, Troy and his stupid crew were MIA, and my dad had finally relaxed. After the police sat down and spoke to him the night of the break-in, he finally chilled, then of course, he went ballistic because I didn't tell him about the threatening phone calls. It took him about a minute and a half to realize that's what I came to him earlier to talk about. He offered to get me a new phone. I declined on principle. Of course I was grounded again for sneaking out. Or rather, his version of grounded. Yeah, I'm still laughing about that, too.

I didn't sleep in my bedroom because it was still a mess.

I just went up there to grab clothes in the morning before school and that's it. I slept in my mom's old bedroom on the second floor. Whenever I did go upstairs, I just shook my head. I know Jalisa and Diamond volunteered to help clean with me. Even Terrence wanted to help, but I turned everybody down. I need to do this myself. But Terrence still righted the bureau, bed, desk and bookcases in both mine and Jade's rooms. So Saturday morning, I just needed to take care of my clothes and books and other stuff like that.

I get up early, shower, dress and go downstairs. My grand-mother left a note on the kitchen table saying she was going out to the grocery store. I grab some orange juice and go back upstairs. When I get to my bedroom it looks even worse than before, if that's even possible. I decide to start in the walk-in closet I share with Jade. That way I can at least put my clothes away as I pick them up.

So I am sitting on the closet floor sorting my shoes when I hear noises in the hall and in Jade's bedroom. I know my grandmother is out, so of course I think whoever was there before had come back. I freeze and look around for something to swing. Then I hear my name called quietly. It's Jade. "Hey," I holler from the closet. "I'm in here."

She peeks inside and looks down. "Hey," she says. "Girl, you scared me. I looked in your bedroom and nobody was there. Then, as I was walking down the hall, I heard a bumping noise."

I hold up a pair of my boots. "I know. You scared me, too. I'm just trying to get the closet straight so we can hang our clothes up again."

She comes in and leans back against one of the built-in dressers. "I guess we had the same idea—Saturday morning cleanup. Who picked up all the big furniture?" she asks, looking back into her bedroom.

"Terrence did," I say. "He came back up Tuesday night after you went back to the dorm and everybody else left."

"Thank him for me," she says.

"You'd better do that yourself. I don't think he's speaking to me anymore."

"Why not? What happened?"

I shrug. "I don't know. He's pissed at me, but I don't know why. All I can think of is maybe it's because he was fighting Darien and had to go to the police station that night. But the day after, we talked and he was okay. Then a few days later he wasn't."

"Something happened in those few days," she surmises.

"I guess, but I don't know what, and he's not saying. Do you know some girl named Gia?"

"Ms. Lottie's granddaughter?" she asks.

"Yeah, they had a thing and broke up just before mom and I came to live here. Now they're both at Howard and I think it's back on again. I think I'm getting played."

"That doesn't sound right," she says.

"Have you ever seen them on campus together?"

"The campus is huge. I've only ever seen Terrence in the library or in the cafeteria when he's working or maybe when his frat is doing something."

"The night all this happened, he got mad again, but I was only trying to protect him."

"What do you mean, protect him from what?"

I look at Jade, not sure if I should tell her, but I have to tell someone. "He was there the night of the robbery at Giorgio's. He was one of them."

"Terrence?" she questions. I nod. "No, that's not possible. I know Terrence. It's not his character. I used to babysit him years ago. He'd never do anything like that, ever."

"But I saw him. And also Li'l T saw him. When we talked at school, he said he recognized one of the guys, too."

"Then he recognized someone else," she says.

All of a sudden I am feeling weird. I should be the one defending Terrence unconditionally like Jade is, instead of accusing him and then trying to protect him. "One of the guys that night had his exact same tattoo in the exact same place on his neck. And don't say I didn't see it because I know I did."

"Kenisha, there are a million guys with the same tattoo in the same place. It doesn't mean they're all guilty. Besides, his frat had some event all Saturday night. I know he had to be there for that."

Everything she is saying made sense. And so now it looks like I have been jumping to the wrong conclusions again. I shrug. It's all messed up.

"It'll work out," she says, reassuringly.

"Like you and Ty?"

She looks away. "That's a whole other story."

"Is it going to have a happy ending?"

She looks back at me and shrugs. "I really don't know." Then she looks away again and her jaw drops. "Kenisha

Lewis, I know you are not wearing my brand-new shoes that I haven't even worn yet."

Oops. I look down at my feet. "Yeah, I tried some of your shoes on. Girl, I had no idea you had all these designer shoes and handbags and stuff in here—Manolo Blahnik, Jimmy Choo, Michael Kors, Dolce & Gabbana," I say. "You have sunglasses, belts, scarves, hats, for real, so you know we wear the same size shoe, right? I'm seriously raiding your side of the closet from now on."

"Not if you want to live to be seventeen," she jokes. She looks down at her rows and rows of footwear. They are all neatly placed below where her clothes are gonna go again. "Thanks for getting them all back together."

"Sure," I say.

"Look, about what I said before when I snapped at you…"

"Jade, I know you were upset about the Tyrece thing. I would be, too. So seriously, don't worry about it." She nods and turns to leave. "Oh, wait, guess what? I checked our jewelry from Mom," I say. Her eyes get wide as she looks over at the bathroom vanity. Then she seems crestfallen and shakes her head. "No, that's just it, they didn't touch anything. I guess a drawer full of tampons and pads is like kryptonite to criminals."

We laugh. "So now, instead of pepper spray, I'll carry some tampons in my bag and just throw them if someone steps up to me."

"Nah, definitely still carry the pepper spray," I say.

"I still can't believe all this," she says miserably.

"I know. It's so stupid. What the hell were they looking for? I swear I don't have anything of Darien's."

"Maybe you hit him too hard with his stupid trophies and broke more than just his arm," Jade jokes. I stop and look up at her. "What?" she asks, seeing the expression on my face.

"Oh, my God," I say.

"What?" she asks again.

"The trophy, I forgot all about it. The police asked if he gave me a box or something, but he didn't. Then when I talked to Ursula before, she said…oh, my God, I know what's in it." I jump up and run into my bedroom. Jade follows. I look under the bed. "I threw it under here."

"You threw what under there?" she asks. I am on my hands and knees, but can't find it by feeling around. So I get up and shift the bed aside. Jade helps. "What are you looking for?" she asks.

"It's not here," I say. "They must have taken it."

"Who took what?"

"Darien's trophy. That night, I hit him twice and each time the trophy broke. Then the last time, I grabbed another one to hit him again, but he was down on the floor. I just took it and ran. Then I remember Ursula said the police found drugs on the floor in his bedroom. He'd been hiding the drugs in the trophies. See, that's what they were looking for. I still had one of his trophies."

"Well, at least they got it now and it's out of here."

"No," I say. "I remember now. I moved it from under the bed." I stand up and walk over to the bedroom door and close it. The trophy is still sitting where I put it days ago. I pick it up and bring it back to where Jade is sitting on my bed.

"Do you think it has drugs in it?" she asks. I nod. She reaches for it, and I move it away. "No, don't touch it."

"Why not?"

"Because when we give it to the police and they dust it for fingerprints, I don't want yours on it."

"Yours are on it," she says.

"Yeah, that's because I was gonna hit him with it. I'm sure they will expect to see that when I explain what happened and why I still have it."

"Do you have any gloves?"

"Yeah, I just put my winter hats, scarves and gloves away in the closet." I run and bring back two pairs of leather gloves. We put them on and search the trophy for an opening. We look for a while, but can't find one. "Why don't I just throw it across the room? It'll be like the rest of the place."

"Except the police are going to know this is what they were looking for, so why would they break in and then leave it here."

"They won't know what kind of condition it was in when I took it from Darien's room," I say.

"True. Okay, do it. But don't make it too badly broken."

I nod and toss it kinda hard across the room. We run over to see if it broke. It didn't. "Maybe there's nothing inside," I say. Then, when I pick it up, I feel the top is loose. I wiggle and twist the silver football figure on top. It turns. I look at Jade. This is it. We sit down on the bed again as I keep untwisting until the whole top part comes loose. Jade holds the base, and I pull the top. It comes apart and all of a sudden all these big fat rolls of hundred dollar bills tumble out all over the bed and floor. The trophy is pretty big and it looks like the rolls of money had been stuffed inside all the way to the top.

We look at each other and then down at all the money on my bed and floor. "Oh, my God, how much do you think it is," I ask.

"Too much," she mutters. "We have to call the police."

"Wait, whoever is after this now thinks it's not here, right?" Jade nods and picks up one of the rolls of cash. "They're gonna have to assume that the police took this trophy with the others, right?" Jade nods again, picking up another one. "So really nobody knows we have this money, right?"

Jade shakes her head. "No. Wrong. So don't even think about it. This is the last thing we need in this house."

"But, Jade…"

"No, Kenisha," she insists firmly, grabbing the rest off the floor as I gather up those that fell on the bed with us.

"Aw, man, you are just too damn honest."

"Believe me, it has nothing to do with me being honest and everything to do with not having this here with us. This is drug money. People got hurt for this money."

I nod slowly. I know she's right. But just for a minute I'm really tempted. "So what do we do?"

"We put the money back."

"All of it? Are you sure?" I joke.

Jade smiles. "Yeah, all of it, I'm sure and so are you."

But curiosity gets the better of us. We dump the rest of the rubber-band rolled money out on the bed first. They were jammed inside really tightly. We finally get them all out. There are twenty rolls, and each roll has between seventy-five and eighty one hundred dollar bills each wrapped up tightly in a rubber band. I grab my calculator, and we figure out the approximate total. When the LCD display shows the total, we just look at each other. There is over one hundred and fifty thousand dollars stuffed in the trophy. "That's a lot of money," I say.

Jade nods. "Yeah, like I said, too much money," she says.

"But what if we give it to the police and they keep it?"

"But what if they come back to look for it again?"

We stuff all the money back inside the trophy and screw the top back on. It looks about how it looked before. Now we are just sitting there looking at it. Neither one of us speaks or barely even breathes. "Jade, Kenisha, I'm back," our grandmother calls out from the second floor. We both jump and grab our chests and then burst out laughing. We keep laughing until tears start streaming down our faces. I grab the trophy and put it back behind my door. It is always open, so I guess that's how they didn't find it when they searched my room.

"Hi, Grandmom," Jade calls down, taking the gloves off.

"Hi, Grandmom," I repeat, taking mine off, too.

"I brought some sandwiches in with me. Come on down and get something to eat."

We both say okay, and then look at each other. "So what do we do with that?"

"We'll leave it where it is for right now. We can think about it later, okay?" she says. I nod. "Come on, let's go."

I head to the front stairs, and Jade heads to the back. "Where are you going?" she asks.

I turn, seeing her opening the back stairs closet. I grimace. "I hate those stairs."

"Come on," she insists, as she pushes the shelving away.

"I hate these stairs," I say, following her in darkness.

"Why? It's quick and easy and leads right to the kitchen."

"But it's so dark. I always feel like I'm gonna fall and break my neck coming down this way or like I'm walking down into the pit of hell." She laughs. "I'm serious, it's scary."

"I used to be scared of coming down here, too, but then I guess I got used to it. Mom took me down one time when I was petrified. She helped me get used to them."

"How?" I ask.

"I remember I must have been about nine or ten. She held my hand and told me to just close my eyes, hold tight to the rail and just keep walking. After that, whenever I'd be nervous about walking into the darkness I'd grab the rail tight like I did with her hand, close my eyes and, like she said, I'd just keep walking."

I smile. It was a great story, and for some reason, it does make me feel a lot better about coming down here.

"You remember mom a lot differently than I do."

"She was there to help each of us when we needed her. She still is. Remember that."

"I know. I guess sometimes I forget," I say.

"You're just like her. You're a fighter. Look at what you've been through with Darien and with the Pizza Place."

"Nah, I see Mom more in you. You're so calm and smart about things. You always know exactly what to do, just like her."

"I guess we have the best of her when we really need it."

"Yeah, that's it."

"You know what? Maybe we can talk Grandmom into putting a light switch at the top and connecting it to the bottom. That way the whole area would be illuminated when we need it to be."

"That's a good idea, 'cause seriously, I hate coming down these stairs," I say again. Jade laughs just as she opens the pantry door. Our grandmother is standing at the table emptying a grocery bag. We greet her, then help put the groceries away. Then we all sit down and eat sandwiches and talk.

Jade suggests putting a light in the back stairs, and Grandmom thinks it's a great idea. Then we talk about school. Thankfully, Jade does most of the talking. I don't feel like it. But I should have known my grandmother wasn't gonna let me be quiet for long. "And what are you up to at school, Kenisha?"

"I'm doing okay, hanging in there. Penn isn't all that bad. And actually, one of my teachers was telling me about applying to hopefully be a congressional page next semester."

"Wow, that's wonderful," my grandmother says.

"Hey, congrats, I was a page right before my senior year, too. We can make it a family tradition."

"I am so proud of you girls I could burst with joy. Just keep doing the right things and everything will be okay," our grandmother says. Jade and I look at each other. We know exactly what she means. "So how's it going upstairs?" she asks as we clean up the kitchen.

"It's going pretty good," I say. Jade agrees.

"Was anything broken?" she asks.

"Nothing that really matters," Jade adds.

"Do you need any help?"

"No, we're okay. We got it."

"Well, I'm going to head on over to the hospital and then…"

"The hospital?" I repeat nervously. "Why, what's wrong?"

"With me, nothing. Are you okay?"

"Why are you going to the hospital?"

"You know I visit friends in the hospital and the nursing home on Saturdays before I go to bingo."

"Oh, that's right. I forgot," I say.

So after lunch and cleaning up the kitchen, my grandmother goes to visit her friends, and Jade and I go back to work upstairs. A few hours later, we finish cleaning and putting our rooms back to normal. We rearranged the furniture and both rooms looked great. Basically, I helped Jade with hers and she helped me with mine. After a while they were as good as new. Actually, better than new.

Later Jade is exchanging clothes out to go back to the

dorm. I sit on her bed while she packs. "So, you don't have to tell me this if you don't want to, but is there any possibility that you and Tyrece could be hooking up again?" I ask.

Jade turns and looks at me, only half smiling. "Well, check you out, getting all up in my business."

I smile, knowing she is joking. "Nah, it's not that. I was just kinda looking forward to being a bridesmaid."

"I don't know if I'm gonna be able to help you with that."

"That's okay, I was just asking."

"So what are you doing the rest of the day?" she asks.

"Nothing. I'll probably call Jalisa and Diamond and see if they want to hang."

"Did you need a ride to your dad's house?"

"Nah, things are too weird there."

"What do you mean?" she asks.

"Oh, my God, I have to show you this." I run into my bedroom and grab my cell phone. I start the video playback application as Jade sits down on the bed. We watch, laughing the whole time. When it is over, we watch it again, laughing the whole time.

"So what did your dad do?" Jade asks.

"He scared that guy to death. He ran out of there quick. But so far he's not doing anything about Courtney. She keeps begging for forgiveness and saying it wasn't her fault, but he's just ignoring her. I don't get it."

"Sure you do. Now he can do anything he wants to do and she can't say or do a damn thing about it. Think of it as a lifetime get-out-of-jail-free card."

"Oh, man, you're right, that's it. He's never gonna be home from now on." I close my phone and turn it off.

"You're still not using your phone. Why? Have you gotten any crank calls the last few days?" Jade asks.

"I don't know. My phone is usually off."

"Look and see."

I turn it on again. As soon as I do, the white message light begins blinking. I open the message application and review the recent ones. "I have four missed calls and a text message from Diamond."

"Who are the missed calls from?"

I press a couple of buttons. "They're all from Diamond, Jalisa, Ursula and my dad."

"Nothing from anyone else?" she asks.

"No, and nothing from the private caller," I say.

"Good, sounds like maybe they gave up," Jade says.

"Yeah, I hope so."

"The other day, you obviously had something to tell me when you came to me. I wasn't hearing anything before. I am now. What's going on? What did you need the money for, school?"

"No, for hospital bills."

"What hospital bills?"

"Grandmom has all these hospital bills. What's up with that?"

"What hospital bills?" Jade repeats, frowning more.

Seeing her expression, I can tell she has no idea what I'm talking about. "They're bills from the Northern Virginia Health Institute. They're, like, for thousands of dollars. Is there something wrong? When was she in the hospital?"

"I've never known her to be in the hospital or even sick. Where'd you see these bills?"

"I saw them in the big envelope on the kitchen table. They were originally sent to Mom in Virginia and now they're here."

"Did you ask her about them?"

"Yeah, she just blew me off. I tried calling the customer service number, but it was a recording." I pull out my cell phone, find the number, then hit redial, then hit the speaker button so she can hear the other end ringing. A few seconds later, the machine comes on again. It lists several options. Jade presses the zero button for more information. An operator comes on.

"Hi," Jade says. "Could you tell me what your hospital specializes in?"

"Yes, cardiovascular medicine."

"Thank you," Jade says, then presses the end call button.

"Um, Courtney said that mom left some insurance policies. Is that true?"

"Yes."

"Who gets them?"

"We do. You, me and Grandmom."

"How? When do we get it?"

"It's for college."

"So you're already using yours?"

"No. I have a full scholarship."

"So, can we maybe take some of your money and my money and pay the hospital bills off?"

"I don't know, maybe, but first we need to find out what's

really going on with this hospital thing. Let me see what else I can find out," she says. I nod. "Okay, I'm ready to go. You sure you don't want a ride to your dad's house or to Virginia to hang with your friends?"

"Nah, I have a ton of homework to do and a lot of reading."

She grabs her bag, laptop and purse. "You gonna be okay here by yourself until Grandmom gets back tonight?" she asks.

"Yeah, no biggie," I say, more calmly than I really feel.

"Okay," she says, then heads downstairs. When she gets to the foyer, she turns. I am on the last step. It always makes a loud squeaking sound when someone steps exactly in the middle. I bounce a couple of times, making the squeak louder and more annoying.

"You know you're only making that worse by doing that," she says. I start chuckling and bounce some more. She shakes her head. "You are such a brat sometimes."

"Yeah, I know and you love it."

"Yeah, whatever," she says, but we both know it's true. We drive each other crazy, but we are still sisters and love it. "Now, call me if you want or need anything," she says.

"Does that include your Manolo Blahniks, too?" I joke.

"Hell, no," she says smiling. "I'll lock myself out. See you later."

"'Kay, see ya." I head to the kitchen as I hear her double lock the front door. I grab some orange juice, some homemade chocolate chip cookies and the Style section of the newspaper and sit down. I drink my juice and eat my cookies while I flip through the paper. There is nothing much in it except how somebody got arrested for something and was getting off easy. I think about Darien. I can't believe he was out on bail after everything he did.

I don't feel like reading this anymore. I fold the paper and rinse out my glass. I grab a bottle of water from the refrigerator, then toss my napkin at the trash can. I usually hit it, but this time I miss. It fell behind the trash can against the back door. I move the can and drop it in.

I look at the pantry door. It would be so easy just to run up the back stairs since the stairs and closet door are right next to my bedroom, but I seriously don't want to go through all that. I take the front stairs, squeak and all.

I don't feel like television or music, so I just sit there in the quiet. I think about filling out my application to be a congressional page, but I'm not in the mood, so I just look it over. I have to write an essay about the most significant change in my life. I nearly laugh out loud. I have about twenty since last summer began. I am not in the mood for that, either. I grab my recipe book and flip through. That's when I hear the first bang. I know exactly what it is. The trash can just fell over. *Shit.* Somebody just opened the back door.

CHAPTER 20

Three's Company

"I've always heard 'out of the frying pan into the fire.' Yeah, I know what that means. So now that I'm in the fire, where do I go next?"

—Twitter.com

okay. My heart is pounding like a jackhammer. I'm shaking all over and I can't stop myself. Now my breathing is getting crazy. I haven't needed my inhaler in a long time. I'm not sure I even know where it is. I stop and listen. I don't hear anything more from downstairs, but I still know somebody is here in the house. I quickly grab my purse and dump it on the bed. My inhaler falls out last. I take a deep breath and almost instantly my lungs clear.

I tiptoe over to my bedroom door and push it to almost closed. I immediately see the trophy. I grab it and hold it to swing, and then it hits me. If they want it, they can have it. I tiptoe back over and sit it down on the floor between my dresser and my desk. They have to see it there. Then I go back to the bedroom door and peek out. I still don't hear anything. Now I am thinking maybe this is all just my imagination. That's when I hear it, the squeak.

I back away from the door and look around. My phone is on the bed where I dumped everything. I grab it and look around again, hearing a second squeak. I know there has to be at least two people. I can't fight two. I need to get out of here. I open my bedroom door more, then ease around to the closet door. Now I hear talking, or more like arguing. They are coming up to the second floor. I open the closet door and push the shelves aside. They roll easily like they always do. But I swear I never remembered them making a noise before.

I duck inside quickly, then close the door and push the shelves back in place. I know not a lot of people outside of the family know about our back stairs, and those who do probably have no idea how to make the shelves slide. So I feel safe enough for right now. But I hear real talking now. One guy is asking someone else about my bedroom. "It's on the third floor, come on."

"Shut up, man, be quiet."

"Man, ain't nobody here. Your girl's always in Virginia on Saturdays and I saw the old lady and her fine-ass sister leave."

I start down a couple of steps, then almost trip. I catch myself, stop and sit down. I do not want to fall. I press the button on my phone to call for help. A small area in the darkness instantly illuminates. I forgot all about that part. I dial 911 and tell the operator in a whisper what is going on. I also tell her about Detectives Clark and Wilson. A few seconds later, I hear Detective Clark. The operator was somehow able to connect me to him. "Kenisha, we're on the way to the house. Where are you?"

"I'm hiding upstairs," I whisper.

"Okay, can you get out of the house without being seen?"

"I don't know, maybe."

"Can you tell how many there are inside?"

"At least two, I think, but maybe…"

The closet door upstairs opens. I stop talking and look up, thinking maybe they heard me. Then I hear them talking again. "No, not that door, this one here," another deep voice says. The closet door closes.

"Kenisha. Kenisha, are you there?"

"Yeah," I whisper again.

"Okay, try to get out of the house."

"I don't have my keys and the front door has a deadbolt lock on it."

"How did they get in? Do you know?"

"I think by the back door."

"Okay, can you get down the stairs to the back door without them seeing you?"

I look around in complete darkness except for the phone's light. I keep pressing the button to keep it lit. "Yeah, maybe. I think I can."

"Good, go now. Be careful. When you get outside I want you to go to a neighbor's house and don't move, understand? We'll find you."

"Okay," I say, hearing my voice trembling.

"Now wait, don't hang up. I'll be right here with you the whole time. We're on our way. Detective Wilson and

I are going to wait at the back door for them to come out. We'll pick them up then."

"Okay," I say again, my voice trembling even more now. I take a deep breath and think about what Jade told me about our mom helping her climb down the stairs. I stand up slowly, grab the rail really tight like I'm holding my mom's hand and just start walking in the darkness. Even before I know it, I am standing in the pantry. I think about turning the lights on, but decide not to just in case there is someone on the lookout in the kitchen.

I listen at the door and don't hear anything. Then I open it slowly and peek out. There is trash all over the kitchen floor where the trash can had been knocked over. I look at the back door. It's pushed but not completely closed. I open the panty door all the way and stand in the kitchen. I hear the squeak on the front stairs again. There is somebody down here still. I tiptoe to the back door, open it, and, just as I am closing it, I hear another voice. "Come on, come on, hurry up, ya'll taking too long," the girl's voice says. I stop. *Ursula?*

I don't know how long I stand there trying to figure out the voice. I'm not really sure. Then it hits me that I have to run. I look around. Nobody is outside. I run to Terrence's house. I know his grandmother is home this time of day. I climb over the fence and run to their back door. I knock, then I bang. Terrence opens the door. He looks at me like I am crazy. "Girl, what the hell are you doing here banging on the door like that?"

"I need help," I say, breathlessly. He looks at me hard. I

hate seeing this look. I know he doesn't like me anymore. "Look, whatever. I just need to be here until it's over."

"Until what's over?" he asks.

"Terrence, there are some police cars out front next door," his grandmother says, coming into the kitchen. She sees me and I guess sees my panicked expression. "Get her inside here now," she says. Terrence grabs my arm and pulls me inside.

I am still shaking when his grandmother comes over to me. "Good Lord, child, what's going on? You're shaking like a leaf."

Terrence goes to open the back door and I grab and push him aside. "No, don't go out there," I yell.

He looks at me, then down at the phone in my hand. "Who's on the phone?"

I stand with my back against their back door blocking him from leaving. Then I hear my name being called over and over again. I put the phone to my ear. "Hello," I say.

"Are you safe?" some woman asks.

"Yeah, I'm next door."

"Good, stay there."

I nod. "Mrs. Harrison, can I stay here with you for a few minutes?" I ask.

"Good Lord, of course."

"What's going on?" Terrence asks.

"There's someone in the house."

"Where are your grandmother and sister?" Mrs. Harrison asks.

"My grandmom is out and Jade just went back to school. I was in the house by myself when I heard them."

"They didn't see you leaving?" I shake my head, no.

There is a loud commotion outside. I jump. Terrence pulls me away from the door. "Stay here," he says, then opens the back door. He steps outside. Mrs. Harrison follows. I want to, but I can't move. I just stay there in their kitchen. I hear my name again. "Yeah, hello," I say.

"Kenisha, where are you?"

"Next door at Mrs. Harrison's house," I say.

"It's over. We got them coming out of the house."

"Okay, thank you," I say, then hang up. I sit down at the kitchen table and just stare. I don't even want to know who it was. I don't care. I know whoever it was found the trophy and that's what they wanted. So good. They got it back, and now Jade and I don't have to think about it anymore.

Terrence comes back in after a while. "You okay?" he asks, sitting down across from me.

"Yeah," I say. I look up at him. He is half-smirking, shaking his head. "What?" I say.

"Girl, you got so much drama around you."

"Yeah, tell me about it. Did they get them for real?"

"Yeah, the cops caught both of them coming out of the house."

"Both?" I question, wondering about the female voice I heard before I closed the back door.

"Yeah, it was your boy Darien and some other dude. They had that trophy you used before to beat him down with them." Then Terrence starts laughing. "That's some messed up stuff right there. Those trophies keep getting his stupid ass in trouble."

"Yeah, I guess so. I didn't even realize I still had it until

I was cleaning up earlier. I gotta call my grandmother and Jade."

"Yeah, and I think the police want to talk to you, too. I'm going back outside."

I call Jade and my grandmother and tell them what happened. After I assure them I am fine and tell them where I am, they tell me they are already on the way. I end the call, and a few minutes later, Diamond calls. "Hey, let me call you right back. We need to talk."

"No, but wait," Diamond says. "I gotta tell you this real fast, then we can talk about it later. Barron came over last night. He was all upset. He told me that it was Troy and some of the other football players who were doing the break-ins around in your neighborhood."

"What?" I say.

"But it wasn't them that did the one at the Pizza Place. Whoever it was scared the hell out of Troy and his boys, 'cause they're not doing it anymore."

"Did he believe them?"

"Yeah."

I hear talking outside. "Let me call you right back." As soon as I end the call, Detective Clark walks in with my grandmother and Terrence's grandmother. I jump up and hug my grandmother. It is so good to see her.

"Kenisha, are you okay?" Detective Clark asks. I nod. "I need to ask you some questions about what happened this afternoon." I nod again. Just then, Jade comes in with Detective Wilson. We look at each other and I start crying. She grabs me and holds tight. After a while, Detective Clark suggests he can talk to me later. But I don't want that. I want to get this day over with.

"Are you sure you're up for this?"

"Yes," I say strongly.

"Okay, take me through it. What happened?"

I tell him about the trash can and how I accidently left it in front of the back door and how I heard it fall when I was in my room. Then I tell him about the creaking step and sneaking out the back way. I debate about telling him I heard a female voice. In the end I decide to tell. What the hell, whoever she was, she was in my house and didn't belong there.

"Did you recognize any of the voices?"

"I didn't hear anybody clear enough to be one hundred percent sure."

"Okay, as I said before, we did arrest two men coming out of your house, Mrs. King. They were carrying a trophy. Do you know where it came from?"

She looks puzzled. "A trophy?"

"That was me," I say quickly. "A few weeks ago Darien Moore and I got into it in his room. He told me his sister was missing. I went to help, but he tried to make me stay. I grabbed one of his trophies and hit him with it. Then I grabbed another one and broke his arm. After that I grabbed another one. When I saw he was incapacitated, I still held on to the trophy and ran."

"I see. So, it's his property. You took it from his house."

"Uh-huh, I didn't know back then that I broke his arm and I was scared he might still come after me again. So, I took it for protection. I never gave it back. I forgot all about it. I only found it when I was straightening up my bedroom after the first time they broke in."

"That was apparently what they were looking for."

"A stupid trophy, that's silly," Jade says, looking directly at me. "Why break into someone's house just to get a trophy? It can't be of that much value."

"Maybe it's sentimental value," I say. "I shouldn't have taken it in the beginning."

"You were defending yourself, it's understandable. So you hit him with his own trophy and broke his arm." I nod. The detectives glance at each other and halfway smile. "Okay, we're gonna wrap this up and let you all get back to what you were doing. If we have any more questions we'll contact you later. Thank you for being so patient. And, Kenisha, you did a really brave thing today."

I nod. I don't really care anymore. They have the trophy and he has his money. It's over for me. If the police open the trophy and find the money, it's on him. Thank God.

CHAPTER 21

The Next Best Thing

"When all is said and done I guess nobody ever really wins in the end. Maybe just breaking even is good enough. All I know is that either way, I'm gonna keep moving forward. Every day is something new and every day I'm gonna deal with it the best way I can. I don't know what's up with tomorrow. I guess I'll see when I get there."

—MySpace.com

WE go to church Sunday morning, then go out afterward and eat brunch. It's just the three of us and it's great. I feel normal again. We drive by Giorgio's, and I see he's in there with his two cooks, but it still isn't open. I get out to say hi, and to tell him I'm not working there anymore. I knock on the locked door, and he walks over and lets me in.

"Hey, how are you?" I say.

"Fine, and you?" he answers, looking around behind me.

I turn to see what he is looking at. "Oh, that's my grandmother and sister in the car waiting for me. I just wanted to stop by to say how sorry I am about everything that happened and to tell you I can't work here anymore."

"I understand."

"Are you going to stay open?"

"Yes."

"Good. Well, I'm gonna go now. I'll be back for pizza. Take care."

"You, too," he says, looking around before unlocking the glass door. He lets me out then locks up immediately and hurries to the back. I guess I really don't blame him for being so skittish. If I had a black eye and a huge busted lip I would be skittish, too.

So I get back in the car and we go home. As soon as we pull in front of the house, we see a big black SUV parked out front, too. We get out and start walking up the path to the front porch. The car door opens and Tyrece, Jade's ex-fiancé, gets out and walks over. "Hello," he says.

"Hi, Ty," I say, happy to see him and knowing this has to be a good sign. He leans down and hugs me and my grandmother. Then he looks at Jade. "Hello, Jade."

"Hello, Ty," she says curtly.

"Grandmom, come on, we should go inside," I say.

We start inside, and I look back, seeing Jade and Ty following. I am hoping she isn't going to do something like slam the front door in his face. Thankfully, she doesn't. We go inside and Jade and Ty stay out on the front porch talking.

To keep busy, Grandmom mixes up a batch of monster cookies, and I bring my laptop down and start outlining what I want to write my congressional page essay on. We are talking in the kitchen when Jade comes back in the house about an hour later. She isn't smiling. "Everything okay?" Grandmom asks.

She shrugs. "Maybe. We'll see. Ty needed to make a quick run to his mom's house. He said he'd be back later." She looks at me. I am smiling so wide my face starts to hurt. That is the best news I've heard in a while. "What are you smiling about?" she asks.

"Nothing, everything," I say. She knows what I mean.

The doorbell rings a few minutes later. Detectives Clark and Wilson come by with a few last-minute questions. Basically, they want to know how I got down the steps without being seen. My grandmother goes to open the pantry door, and I take them up to the closet next to my bedroom. When they come back down the back stairs, they are chuckling. We sit down in the living room, and they tell us the man with Darien has a slash on his hand and they suspect he is the same man from the Giorgio's break-in and the others. They're testing his blood against the blood on the pizza cutter for a match.

"Who is he?" Jade asks.

"Nobody, just someone trying to make a name for himself."

"And the others in the robbery?" I ask.

"We don't have any leads right now. If you think of anything, let us know." I nod, but I know I'm not going to think of anything. Afterward, they thank us again for our help, then leave.

They are leaving when my dad, Cash and the boys are walking up the steps. My dad shakes hands with the detectives in greeting. I know I have to tell him what happened the day before. I'm just not looking forward to it. They come in. The boys hug me and Jade then make a beeline to the kitchen to find my grandmother. Jade and Cash follow.

"Why were the detectives here?" my dad asks.

"Sit down, Dad," I say. I tell him what happened, how I slipped down the back stairs and ran out. He nods a lot, but keeps quiet mostly. He asks a few questions and is surprised we even have back stairs. "Are you okay?" he finally asks when I am finished.

"Yeah, I'm fine. All that's finally over," I say.

"Do you want to come back to Virginia to live? You can go to Hazelhurst if you want. That's why I came by. I paid the tuition last Friday."

"Nah, get your money back. I'm staying at The Penn."

"I always hated that nickname."

"Really, I kind of like it now."

He frowns. "Are you sure? What about all your friends?"

"They're still my friends. That part will never change."

"I'll tell you what. I'll leave the tuition there at the school in an escrow account, just in case you change your mind in your senior year."

"Thanks, Dad. What about you, are you okay after all that?"

"Yeah, I'm good."

"We got stuffed monster cookies," Jason says, with his face smeared with chocolate. "Grandmom said to come get a cookie, too."

Dad and I go to grab a cookie. We talk a few minutes, then Ty comes back. Jade introduces everyone. My dad and Cash are stunned when he walks in. I guess it's not every day a Grammy Award-winning, multi-platinum album-receiving, worldwide entertainer walks in the kitchen and just grabs a cookie and gets milk from the refrigerator and starts chatting like it's no big deal. The fact that he insists on calling me Lil Sis really trips them out. After a while, Jade and Ty leave. Then my dad and everybody leaves.

Later that evening, my grandmother is up in her bedroom, and I am sitting out on the back porch chilling. After everything is done, and all the questions are answered, it's nice to just sit back and chill. I sit watching the rain come down. It's just getting to be dark, and rumbles of thunder are in the distance. I am texting both Jalisa and Diamond and not paying attention to anything else.

"Hey."

I jump, then calm down instantly hearing the familiar voice. I look over, seeing Terrence on his back porch, too. What was I thinking? Tattoo or not, that definitely wasn't lawn mower guy's voice before. "Hi," I say. I tell my girls that lawn mower guy is here and I'll catch up with them later. I get two smiley faces. I watch as he runs over, hops the fence and hurries to our porch. I stand waiting. "You're wet," I say.

"No biggie."

"Are we ever gonna be okay again?" I ask.

"I don't know. I have to think about it. I still can't believe you thought that was me at Giorgio's," Terrence says.

"I'm sorry. I just saw the tattoo and it scared me."

"But you think I'd do that and beat up on some guy?"

"No, never. It's just that after that Gia thing, we weren't really talking and I had no idea what was going on with you."

"So you believed the worst of me."

"I believed that I needed to protect you," I say.

He nods. "For the record, I was stuck at work all day Saturday. Then the brothers at the frat did a fundraiser on campus for sickle cell anemia. I was there all night."

"I know it wasn't you."

"Good, I can't believe you actually thought I'd rob the Pizza Place."

"Momentary insanity," I say.

"Yeah, that I can believe," he jokes.

"I gotta find Li'l T and straighten his butt out," I say.

"I already talked to him. He thought it was funny that you thought it was me."

"So who did he recognize?"

"He said it was your girl's brother. He thought that's why you were so upset and who you were protecting. Some dude named Brian. He's a crackhead who lives around the way."

There was another jolt to my system. "Brian, Jalisa's big brother?" I ask.

He shrugs. "I don't know."

"Okay, since we're clearing the air, what was up with you and Gia? I mean I get it, she's older and you go to the same school and all, but…"

"What are you talking about?"

"She said that you two hang out at school."

"Yeah, we do. I tutor her. That's one of my jobs."

"*One* of them?" I ask.

"I have three," he says.

"You have three jobs? How? Why?"

He takes a deep breath and sighs heavily. "The fight I was in with D a few weeks ago messed up one of my scholarships. To stay in school I had to make up the money somehow. I tutor, I work in the cafeteria and I work in the bookstore."

"That's why you never come home anymore."

"Yeah."

"Why didn't you just tell me all this before?" I ask.

"I was pissed."

"It was my fault."

"No, it wasn't. I chose to fight D. We've been going at this thing for years."

"Still, if you hadn't seen me that night, you'd still have your scholarship money. So it is my fault."

"I've already applied for another scholarship for next semester. Financial aid said it looks really good."

"So maybe you won't have to work then?" I ask hopefully.

"Nah, I'm still keeping at least one of the jobs."

"Maybe not tutoring," I suggest.

"You're sounding a little jealous, girl."

"I know, right," I say.

"Well, don't be," he whispers. Then he kisses me and I kiss him right back. And all of a sudden, everything feels all right again. We stay out a little while longer talking. Then he has to get back to Howard, and I need to get ready for school the next day. We say goodbye and make plans to catch up the following weekend. We wave as we both go back into the houses.

I feel like I just lived a lifetime in the last three weeks. I take the back stairs up to my bedroom. Tomorrow is Monday, and I need to get my head straight for that. I am going to school and have no intention of hiding at Dr. Tubbs' office.

I sit on my bed with my laptop open to the congressional page application on one side of me and my recipe book on the other. I pick up and flip through the recipe book. I read all the things I've been through since I came to live here with my grandmother and my sister. Dad asked if I wanted to move back to Virginia and go to my old school again. There's no way I can do that. My phone beeps, then my text message light blinks. I pick it up and press the button to see the message.

From: Lawnmower Guy ...yeah, we're good!

I start laughing. Crazy and insane, I love my life here now. This is home. I learn something new every day and tomorrow, who knows?

★ ★ ★ ★ ★

QUESTIONS FOR DISCUSSION

1. In *Getting Played* Kenisha's grandmother talks about the importance of family—the bond between Kenisha and her sister Jade—and keeping the family together. How does this bond get stronger in the book?

2. In the book there is a robbery at the Pizza Place where Kenisha works. One of the would-be robbers tries to take her hostage. But she quickly figures a way out of the situation. Have you ever faced a situation where you had to use your wits to avoid trouble?

3. Kenisha writes down her hopes, dreams, life lessons and, of course, recipes in her recipe notebook. It becomes a big part of her. What are some of the things you could put in your notebook?

4. The book's title is *Getting Played*. Identify some of the ways you think Kenisha felt like she was being played. By whom? And how?

5. There are some very strong people in Kenisha's life. They guide and protect her when she feels lost or confused. Who are some of the people you have around you and how have they helped you in difficult situations?

6. Kenisha and Jade find a large sum of money in one of Darien's trophies. Kenisha hints that she wants to keep

it, but Jade insists that they turn it in. What would you have done? What's wrong with keeping the money? And could it be dangerous to keep it?

7. Kenisha's locker is next to the locker of the hottest guy at Penn Hall, Troy Carson. Troy's character is complicated. He pretends to be something he's really not. Why do you think he does this? Do you think he'll ever own up to the fact that he's smart?

8. In the story, Kenisha likes to sit perched up high and look down below. She does this in her bedroom and in the private dance room on the top floor at Freeman Dance Studio. Why do you think she does this?

9. In the end, Kenisha decides to stay at Penn Hall and live with her grandmother and Jade, even though she knows there will be more drama in her life. Why do you think she chooses to stay?

10. Ms. Grayson, Kenisha's History teacher, wants to help Kenisha with her problems. Do you think Kenisha will ever open up to her?

11. Kenisha can be strong, determined, selfish, thoughtful and resourceful. What character traits of Kenisha's do you share and why?

12. Kenisha is still struggling to accept her mother's death. Do you think Kenisha will ever accept Courtney as a mother-figure in her life? Why or why not?

13. Kenisha finds herself in the wrong place at the wrong time. Why is it always important to be aware of your surroundings?

14. Kenisha finds out that her best friend, Jalisa, has been hit by her boyfriend. She is shocked and hurt. She feels she should have been there for her friend. How would you handle the situation if it was your best friend?

KRYSTAL JUST MET THE PERFECT BOY.
TROUBLE IS, HE'S DEAD.

MANIFEST

ARTIST ARTHUR

Book #1 in the new Mystyx series...

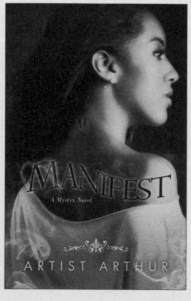

Krystal Bentley is an outsider at her new high school, having just moved to a small Connecticut town. Lately she's been hearing the voice of teenage murder victim Ricky Watson in her head. As a ghost, Ricky needs Krystal's help to solve the mystery of his murder.

When Krystal befriends two other outsiders at school, they discover each has a unique paranormal ability—and an unusual birthmark in the shape of an *M*. As they form their "Mystyx" clique, they work to solve Ricky's murder and understand the mystery behind their powers.

On Sale July 27, 2010, wherever books are sold.

www.KimaniTRU.com
http://www.facebook.com/pages/Kimani-TRU/20282714482
www.myspace.com/kimani_tru
http://twitter.com/kimani_books

KPAA1960810TR

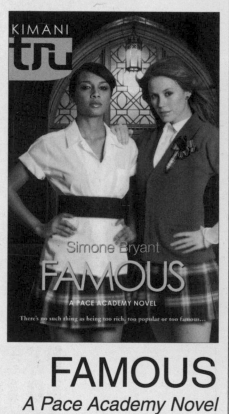

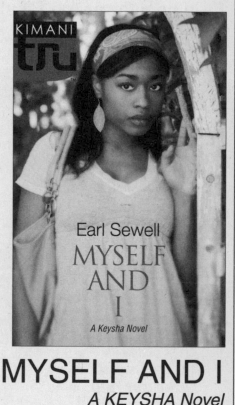